W9-BXD-236

4 1/2 Friends

and the
Disappearing Bio Teacher

Joachim Friedrich

Translated from the German
by Elizabeth D. Crawford

Hyperion Books for Children
New York

For Daniela, Janine, and Christopher

Translation © 2001 by Elizabeth D. Crawford
Joachim Friedrich, 4 1/2 FREUNDE UND DIE VERSCHWUNDENE BIO-LEHRERIN
© 1992 by K. Thienemanns Verlag, Stuttgart—Wien
All rights reserved. No part of this book may be reproduced or transmitted in any form or by
any means, electronic or mechanical, including photocopying, recording, or by any information
storage and retrieval system, without written permission from the publisher. For information
address Hyperion Books for Children, 114 Fifth Avenue, New York, New York 10011-5690.

First American Edition
1 3 5 7 9 10 8 6 4 2

Printed in the United States of America

Library of Congress Cataloging-in-Publication Data
Friedrich, Joachim.
[4 1/2 freunde und die verschwundene Biolehrerin. English]
4 1/2 friends and the disappearing bio teacher / Joachim Friedrich; translated from the
German by Elizabeth D. Crawford.
p.   cm.
Summary: Norbert and his friends in the detective club set out to explain the strange
appearance and behavior of their attractive biology teacher.
ISBN 0-7868-0698-2 (trade)
[1. Teachers—Fiction. 2. Schools—Fiction. 3. Germany—Fiction. 4. Mystery and detective
stories.] I. Title: Four and one-half friends and the disappearing bio teacher. II. Crawford,
Elizabeth D. III. Title.
PZ7.F91515 Aaf   2001
[Fic]—dc21   00-49903

Visit www.hyperionchildrensbooks.com

Contents

Like an Angel

SHE HOVERED OVER THE CLASSROOM like an angel. Her face glowed. Something otherworldly emanated from her. Oh, how could a woman be so beautiful?

My heart raced. My head was swimming. And when she spoke, it was music to my ears.

"You are an indescribably lazy bunch of kids!"

She was waving our bio tests like Joan of Arc with her banners. She came toward me. Soon I would feel a gentle breeze when she passed me. She came closer and closer. Now I could smell it—like violets or roses. Whatever it was, I had never smelled anything so wonderful before. And today she was looking even more beautiful than usual.

Not that Ms. Hober-Stratman had been coming to school in tatters before, but she'd always worn ordinary teacher clothes, which, as everyone

knows, aren't particularly chic. When Ms. Hober-Stratman came to our school at the beginning of the year, I thought at first that she was an ordinary teacher. But the better I got to know her, the more certain I became that she was something very special. It was obvious, in spite of the teacher clothes. And for the last few weeks she'd been getting prettier and prettier! Instead of coming in jeans, she always wore dresses now. Each one was more attractive—and probably also more expensive—than the last. It almost seemed to me that she bought a new one for each bio class. She was wearing more makeup than usual—even bright, kiss-red lipstick.

She turned around and came back toward me again. She wobbled a bit, probably because she wasn't used to the high heels. The whole time she kept going on about the bad results on the test. I inched my chair nearer to the aisle and pointed my nose in her direction. At the moment she was passing me, I sucked in the air deeply. Oh, that fragrance! Out of this world!

Ms. Hober-Stratman turned on her heel and snatched me from my thoughts.

"Why are you snuffling so, Norbert? Do I smell bad, or do you have a cold?"

Why can't a person just become invisible when he needs to? But that wasn't the end of it. After Ms. Hober-Stratman waited until the idiots in my class

had quieted down again, she began a renewed attack. She held a paper under my nose. I sensed something bad coming.

"You've stolen the show with an F, Norbert. It isn't the flowers that pollinate the bees, it's the other way around!" The class burst into hysterics again.

Oh, how can a woman be so cruel?

"Quiet!" she bellowed. "The way these tests turned out, none of you has any right to laugh. When we go on our field trip, you're going to wish you knew more about biology. That I can promise you!"

Instantly the laughter turned to groans. Every class that had bio with Ms. Hober-Stratman had to go on a field trip with her. And she always took them hiking in Huntsville. The third-period class had already had their trip. What they had told us made chills run down our spines. Ms. Hober-Stratman tramped through the woods with them for the entire day. She asked them about every blade of grass. Even if we don't particularly like the third-period kids, we felt sorry for them. They were limping for a week, they were so sore.

But that isn't the only reason Ms. Hober-Stratman isn't particularly popular with most kids. As pretty as she is, she's also very strict. But I know she's only pretending to be strict so that

we won't push her around. Beneath her rough exterior beats a soft heart. The others just haven't realized it yet.

Although no one laughed anymore for the rest of the period, I knew the business of the flowers and the bees wasn't over for me by a long shot. It was last period. I shuddered to think of the trip home.

Collin was the first. He didn't even wait until we were out of the classroom. "Hey, Norbert!" he teased as we made our way to the door. "Would you like to go over that stuff about the bees and the flowers again? Or do you still believe that the stork brings babies?"

"Dude! Haven't you ever messed up a test?"

"Nah!" Collin sneered.

I was mad, because he was right. Collin is—besides Steffi—the best in the class, even at sports.

Steffi and Radish were already waiting for me at the gate. Luckily Radish gave me a break. Probably because he has to put up with a lot of teasing himself because of his size. After all, he's almost a head shorter than his twin sister. So we call him Radish, although his name is really Austin Rademacher. But my life isn't much better. When teams are being chosen in gym class, Radish and I are always the last ones to be chosen.

Steffi was as mean as Collin, meaner, actually. She looked at me smugly, grinning from ear to ear. "Well, Norbert!" she asked finally. "Are you in love with Ms. Hober-Stratman?"

"Dude! Are you crazy? How'd you get that idea? That is absolutely not true! Me in love? With her? Never!"

I was thinking back, panic-stricken. Had I acted suspiciously? Or did I perhaps murmur something to myself without even noticing?

Steffi's grin got even broader. "Don't get excited. I was just asking. Besides, my name is Steffi, not 'Dude.'"

At last Radish came to my rescue. "Lay off him, guys. You know he calls everyone 'Dude.' And where did you get the idea that he's in love with Ms. Hober-Stratman?"

"Whenever we have bio, Norbert sits nailed to his chair and looks like a lovesick puppy. And I heard him sigh softly a few times. After all, I sit right behind him."

So that was it! I'd have liked to disappear into thin air.

"Norbert sighed?" howled Collin. "Honest? Oh yeah, he's in love!"

"What garbage!" I yelled too loudly.

"So why did you sigh and look lovesick?"

Ouch! I got hot and cold at the same time. "I didn't sigh. And furthermore, I wasn't looking lovesick but . . ."

"But?"

"I was meditating."

"Well, that's a new one!" Now Radish was in there too. "What were you meditating about? Ms. Hober-Stratman?"

Why shouldn't they know? Maybe they might even have an explanation for it.

"Yes, exactly. About Ms. Hober-Stratman. You see, I think something's wrong with her."

Collin's facial expression changed instantly. He became curious.

"Really, Norbert? Why do you think that?"

Steffi put her fists on her hips. "Now cut it out, Collin. This isn't a case for your detective club"

It took a moment before Collin could answer. He was too mad. "Steffi! How often do I have to tell you that Collin and Co. is a detective agency and not a club! Besides, it isn't just *my* agency. You belong to it, too. And so do Norbert and Radish!"

Steffi's smile vanished. "I know. But we haven't solved any cases. I mean, even our treasure hunt was bogus."

"Don't remind me! But still, that doesn't mean anything. Just because it hasn't happened doesn't

mean it won't. You just have to keep your eyes open. Now, then, Norbert, what's going on with Ms. Hober-Stratman?"

"Haven't you noticed that she's changed lately?"

"No. How do you mean, changed?"

"She's gotten . . . more serious, somehow."

"No wonder," Radish said. "The bio test turned out to be a total disaster."

"Dude! I didn't mean that. She just used to be more lighthearted."

"Since when was Ms. Hober-Stratman lighthearted?" cried Radish. "She's only ever picked on me."

"Right," Steffi agreed. "I can't remember even one joke she's made, and I think she only laughs on holidays."

"Maybe she's worried about something." I offered.

Collin snorted. "Worried! What worries could a teacher have? The only worry she has is how she can torture us with her stupid field trip."

"If she just wouldn't stare like that . . ." said Radish.

Steffi nodded. "No kidding! She could burn holes through a safe with that look."

I knew exactly what look she meant.

"You know, now that you mention it, I *have* noticed something. Have you noticed how she's been dressing up lately?" asked Collin. "Her clothes are getting tighter and shorter all the time. The other day, I saw her almost break her legs cramming herself into her beat-up old car."

"Have you noticed that too? And today she was even wearing perfume!" I cried.

Steffi didn't let an opportunity like that slip by. "Really? How romantic! Nevertheless, I can't stand her. As far as I'm concerned I'd prefer a nice ugly teacher to a mean pretty one. She's a nightmare."

These people had no idea at all. Just because she wouldn't let us push her around, she wasn't a nightmare, by any stretch.

"But it is pretty odd that she's been wearing those attractive dresses and wearing makeup all of a sudden," Collin said thoughtfully.

Steffi knew right away where he was heading. "Forget it, Collin! There's no Case of Ms. Hober-Stratman."

"But why is she behaving so oddly?"

"What's odd about her dressing more attractively? Maybe she's in love."

"Exactly! With Norbert!" Collin burst out laughing.

"Or she won the lottery!" Radish chimed in.

"Then she probably wouldn't work anymore,"

said Collin. "And besides, the first thing she would do would be buy a new car. That one she's driving around in now is only held together by rust."

"If you're so interested in what's going on with her, you can always ask her, Collin," Steffi said.

"Whoa, I'm not crazy!" cried Collin. "You know she freaks out if we ask about her private life. Remember how she shriveled Nadine just because she asked if she was married?"

We remembered very well. Poor Nadine.

"Oh, no," Collin continued, "I'm not setting myself up for that. I'd rather do without a case."

Steffi clapped him on the shoulder. "The first reasonable thing I've heard from you today, Boss."

"Good. Now I can relax and go home."

"I would suggest that too."

I dropped my schoolbag in shock. It was Ms. Hober-Stratman. She was standing right behind us. I prayed that she'd just gotten there. She looked at me and smiled! My throat went dry.

"I didn't realize it was so hard for you kids to separate from school. But if you don't get on your way soon, your parents are going to worry about you." And with that she went on past us across the schoolyard. We looked after her, speechless, as she went to the teachers' parking lot. She looked fantastic!

Only then did I see the car. It was a little bright-red sports car. Ms. Hober-Stratman walked right over and unlocked it, climbed in, and roared away with squealing tires.

"Did you see that?" cried Collin, so loud that his voice cracked. "That was a Porsche! Man!"

"And you just said that the first thing she would do if she won the lottery would be to buy a car," said Radish.

"That was instinct, pal," Collin swaggered.

"Get a grip." Steffi took him right down. "Still, I'm gradually beginning to find this whole thing odd now, myself. First jeans and a rattletrap and now expensive clothes and a sports car."

"Right! In any case we should call a conference about it. I'm thinking this afternoon."

"And where would this conference take place, Collin?" asked Steffi skeptically.

"Always at the home of the person who asks," he replied.

"Not at our house again! No way! We're always meeting in my room so you can play on my computer. You're going to break it some day!"

"So where should we go then?" Collin wanted to know.

Steffi, Radish, and Collin all looked at me at the same time. I wanted to say something, but they beat me to it.

"It can't be at my house!" they cried in unison.

I think I blushed. "Dude! It can't be at my house. I've already told you how small our apartment is. Plus my mother would be there the whole time. She'd totally bother us."

"Man, Norbert!" cried Collin. "I thought your mother worked. Besides, we've never been to your house. I don't even have any idea what your house looks like."

"But it really won't work today. My mother is home today."

"Funny how whenever we have a conference she doesn't have to work."

"Dude! Why don't we do it at your place?"

"We've already been to my house."

"Only twice."

"Yeah, well, you know why. My brother is always coming in and making fun of us."

"Yeah, so? A brother isn't as bad as a parent."

"All right, cut it out," said Radish finally. "Let's just go to our house. We can do it in my room. Nothing will happen to Steffi's computer there."

Steffi gave him a poke in the ribs. "Brother dear, you're much too good-natured, you know that? Okay—but they can't drink our soda. Mom complained about the empty fridge last time."

Collin put on his patronizing air. "I'll donate the

soda. And Norbert can bring some snacks."

He looked at me. What was I supposed to do? I nodded, grateful they weren't coming to my house.

Collin was satisfied. "Then everything is all settled."

I walked home feeling guilty. It was true that Mom was home that day. But only until three o'clock. Then she had to go to work. She had the late shift. I looked at my watch. All the discussion about Ms. Hober-Stratman had made me late. I had to hurry, because Mom insists we at least eat together when she has the late shift. Since Mom and I have been living together alone, she's working in the factory again, the way she used to. "I don't earn much, it's true," she always says, "but at least we're independent."

My dad kept our old big apartment while Mom and I moved into a smaller one. The building is really old, and Mom is always complaining that something or other isn't working, plus the furniture isn't as new and modern as the Rademachers' or at Collin's house. That's why I'm not so eager to have our conferences take place at my house. Collin and the others already make enough fun of me. They don't need to make fun of our apartment, too.

When I opened the downstairs door, Mom was standing upstairs in the door to our apartment.

"Where have you been?" she called to me. "You know I'm on the late shift. We barely have time to eat together."

Once we were inside, she immediately took away my bookbag and hung up my jacket. I really hate that, but I don't say anything anymore. I've already tried a few times, but it doesn't matter, she keeps on doing it.

"Anything special happen at school?" she asked when we were sitting at the table.

I just shook my head.

"So why are you home so late?"

"We had something to discuss."

"You and your friends?"

I nodded. "Collin, Steffi, and Radish."

Mom smiled. "Your detective club, then. Are you meeting them again today?"

"Mhm."

She put down her fork. "I keep meaning to ask you, Norbert. Why don't your friends ever come here? I would love to get to know them better."

I wanted to say something, but I didn't know what. Instead I just shoveled in the food. It tasted so good.

Mom wouldn't let it rest. "Don't you want to invite them over sometime?"

I shrugged my shoulders.

"Norbert, Norbert." She sighed. "Sometimes I have the feeling that I don't have any idea what is going on inside your head."

I didn't look at her. I don't like it when she's like that.

I was glad when she finally went to work without mentioning the subject of friends again. I just managed to get my homework done, or at least most of it, when I had to get going, too. Collin doesn't like it when you're late to conferences. I hurried, although I had no great desire to.

Meetings of a Strange Kind

ON THE WAY TO STEFFI AND RADISH'S I bought some pretzel sticks and peanuts. I had barely enough allowance left for that. It made me mad that I had to spend my last few dollars just to keep from being hassled by Steffi.

I was in a bad mood when I rang the Rademachers' doorbell. Mr. Rademacher's face broke into a wide grin when he saw it was me.

"Hello, Norbert. Another secret conference? You can go right up. The others are already up there."

I didn't say anything. Of course Collin was already there. He always arrives too early when Collin and Co. meet.

"There you are," he greeted me, with a glance at his wristwatch. "And not a moment to spare."

"Better on time than half an hour too early," Steffi countered.

One thing you have to say for Radish's sister, she distributes her shots of poison around evenly.

Collin blushed. "I just wanted to try out your new computer program for a minute."

Steffi nodded. "I know. And then I need two days to get the thing running right again."

"C'mon guys, quit squabbling," Radish broke in. "I thought we were going to talk about Ms. Hober-Stratman."

Collin looked at him gratefully. "Exactly! Radish is right. After all, we're here about a case, not a computer program."

"It's not a case yet," I reminded him.

"Maybe not, but it could turn into one fast. First the expensive clothes, and then the car."

"And why should that turn into a case?" Steffi asked irritably.

"Simple. Because no teacher can afford a car like that, at least not on his or her salary."

"That's right," Radish said. "Our father is a teacher and he's always moaning about how he doesn't earn enough for anything."

"Especially since we bought this house," his sister added.

"Then there are only three possibilities," our

boss declared solemnly. "She won or inherited the money, she borrowed it, or . . . she stole it. Blackmail would be another possibility."

"Dude! Are you crazy? Ms. Hober-Stratman a criminal? Never!"

"Calm down, Norbert. I didn't say she was. But you have to consider all the possibilities. It would be best if we shadowed her for a while to find out."

Steffi tapped her forehead. "Shadow her? I really am beginning to believe that you've seen too many crime shows on TV. You suspect foul play behind every little thing."

"If you have a better idea, tell us!"

Steffi folded her arms across her chest. "Maybe I don't have a better idea! Maybe you're beginning to get on my nerves! I have no desire to talk any more about imaginary cases, and I really, really have no desire to shadow Ms. Hober-Stratman. If she catches us, she'll shrivel us up so small that we'll all fit into a shoe box together."

"But—" Collin tried once more.

"No buts! You can shadow Ms. Hober-Stratman all you want, just do it without me!"

With that the Hober-Stratman case was finished for Collin. Of course he didn't say so, but we all know he would rather give up the most exciting case of the century than give up having Steffi in his agency.

We really could have left at that point, but we still had soda and snacks. So we sat there, eating and drinking and talking mostly about school. There was no more mention of Ms. Hober-Stratman. I thought to myself that Radish was probably very relieved. He had definitely been anxious about shadowing our tough bio teacher. I wasn't entirely sure what to think about it. On the one hand, I would have been glad to be near her, and I would also have liked to know why she'd changed so much. On the other, I wouldn't have wanted her to catch us somehow and be angry at me. I felt pretty bad, so I ended up eating most of the peanuts by myself.

"Is there any more soda?" Collin asked finally.

Wordlessly, Steffi showed him the empty bottle.

He got up and gave us all the evil eye. "Well, then, I'm out of here. See you tomorrow at school."

No one tried to stop him. He was almost out the door when he turned around again. "I don't think that's nice of you, Steffi. I really don't."

Steffi shrugged her shoulders. "When you show me that Ms. Hober-Stratman actually is a case, I'll be back on it."

Collin didn't look as though that reassured him.

I stood up, too. That was a mistake.

"Were you going to go, too, Norbert?" Collin asked.

"Yes, I was, actually " I answered.

"Good, then we can go together."

I'd been afraid of that. Not that I had anything against Collin, but I knew him very well, so I knew what was in store for me.

I was right. We were hardly out on the street when he let loose. "What a mean trick!" Collin cried. "Can you tell me why Steffi acted like that all of a sudden?"

I could not. Even if I could have, he wouldn't have listened. He only wanted someone he could moan and groan to. All Steffi has to say is: "Collin, shut your trap!" and he quiets down immediately. I can never get away with that, and it really bothers me. Sometimes it even makes me angry, but I can't confront him. I wish so often that I were like Collin. Everything goes right for him, if you don't count the fact that Collin and Co. has never solved a real case. He's an ace at sports, he's never had worse than a C on his class work, and no one laughs at him, or at least not very often. There probably isn't a girl in our class who doesn't make goo-goo eyes at him—except for Steffi. And that really drives him crazy. He's obsessed with solving a real crime, at least a small one. And he would give anything for Steffi to worship him just like the other girls. But so far neither of these things has happened.

So now his flood of complaints was pouring out, and I just let it roll over me on our trip home. He griped about girls in general and Steffi in particular, complained that no real gangsters were doing their evil deeds in our hick town, ranted and raved about the stupid teachers, and on and on.

My head was buzzing by the time we finally got to the street corner where our paths parted.

"Well, see you tomorrow, Norbert. I feel a lot better now. It's good to be able to say what's on your mind once in a while," he said. He grinned at me, then clapped me on the shoulder, turned, and walked off, whistling cheerfully.

I just stood there, staring after him. *He* felt better. Well, great! First he unloads all his frustration on me and then he leaves me standing there. My spirits were down to absolute zero. I felt as if a big black thundercloud were hanging over my head.

I'd just gone a few steps when I noticed a woman on the opposite side of the street. Somehow she looked familiar, although I couldn't place her. She had light blond hair and was wearing a tight red dress. There was a man walking beside her, and it looked as though they were in a big hurry—almost as if they were running away from somebody. They were a few steps ahead of me, so I couldn't see their faces. I had to almost run to keep up with them. The woman kept looking around as if she wanted to be sure that no one was following them, but it happened so fast each time that I couldn't see her face. She linked arms with the man, probably because she couldn't walk so fast in her high-heeled shoes. Where had I seen that woman before?

Finally they had to wait for a red light. I had to get closer to them. I decided it would be better to switch over to the other side of the street. I started across without looking to the left or right and ran right in front of a guy on a bicycle. He was barely able to stop in time. He was huge and ugly. His face, with ears attached to it that reminded me of giant sails, consisted almost entirely of pimples.

"Why don't you look where you're going, Fatso?" he snarled.

Now, I'm really a very friendly person. But a few things do make me angry, especially when I'm already in a bad mood, and the biggest one is when somebody calls me "Fatso." I know I'm too fat, and I've tried to eat less. But somehow I just can't do it. But that's still no reason to call me names. I could feel the rage rising in me. Normally, I would have been afraid of that giant. But in my fury, I didn't care.

"Dude! Better to be a fatso than a pepperoni pizza with handles!" I bellowed back.

For a moment Dumbo was flabbergasted. Then he pulled himself together.

"What did you say, Piggy-Wiggy?" he yelled as he leaped off his bike. "I'll give you a pair of fat lips for that!"

Luckily, he was so angry that the first thing he did was trip over his bicycle. That gave me some lead time, but not much. I looked around in desperation for a place to hide as I ran for my life. I ran into a little side street where two garbage cans were standing beside a projection in a wall. I crept behind them. The stink was brutal, but I didn't care. My heart was beating so hard I was afraid it would give me away. At that moment I caught sight of two jeans legs with oversized gym shoes underneath them. They could only belong to the ugly giant. He stopped. He was probably looking around. Then he slowly came toward the garbage cans. There were only seconds left. In my mind's eye I saw myself living the rest of my life without teeth.

And then suddenly I felt something soft against my back. It bumped into me a few times and then crawled up under my jacket. My stomach turned over, my heart stopped, and I broke into a sweat, but I couldn't move. At that moment the thing under my jacket began to whistle. What could it be?! I was forced to consider what animals usually lurk in the vicinity of garbage cans. I wasn't pleased with my choices. My insides lurched. Rats! Surely those grisly vermin were just about to start eagerly gnawing on me.

The giant gym shoes came closer. One more step and he'd have me. Just when I'd given up all hope, help arrived. It shot toward me. I could only see four legs, which skidded to a stop just in front of the garbage cans. The dog to which the legs belonged must have been about the size of a calf. He was growling and barking, and I couldn't tell if his furious attack applied to me or to Gym Shoes. I'd never been so scared in my life. A pimple-faced giant was going to clobber me, a dog was probably going to eat me if he found me, and a whistling monster was under my jacket.

"Beat it, you lousy mutt!" the giant bellowed.

The dog barked and growled even louder. At the same moment I heard something clatter and the four dog legs ran away howling. The guy had thrown a bottle or something. I sighed, not only because the dog was gone, but the gym shoes also turned around and disappeared in the direction of the street. So the two enemies had eliminated each other, so to speak. I sighed again. Now there was just the thing under my jacket left to deal with. I listened. It kept on whistling softly. It wasn't a melodious whistling. It sounded more like an old teakettle. Did rats whistle like that? I wasn't sure. There was only one way to find out.

I gathered all my courage. With trembling hands I lifted up my jacket, prepared to look into the maliciously grinning faces of an entire rat family. But what I saw was not rats at all. It was two brown dog eyes! And they were looking at me as though they were even more afraid than I was. When my heart and my stomach had quieted somewhat, I examined my guest a little more carefully. He was quite a small specimen, and his breed was indefinable. He sniffed at me for a while. Then he put his nose right up to my face and took one lick straight across it, and as he did, I could see that he was missing a few teeth. I realized he'd been breathing so fast with excitement and fear that the air was whistling through his missing teeth. I have an uncle who's missing an incisor, and he can whistle the most fantastic tunes through the empty space. I wondered whether a dog could learn something like that if you practiced with him long enough.

I looked for a collar. He wasn't wearing one. It would have surprised me if he had been, he looked so raggedy. His coat was mangy, as if a swarm of moths had feasted on him, and he was missing a piece of his left ear—it had probably been bitten off.

24

"I bet the big dog was after you, huh?" I asked my whistling little friend. In answer he licked all the way across my face again.

"Dude! I guess we pretty much saved each other!"

This time I was just able to avoid the tongue. I removed him from under my jacket and cautiously crept out from behind the garbage cans. The little fellow followed me out, just as cautiously.

"Okay, the coast is clear," I said softly and gave him a little pat on the head. "So, take care of yourself. Maybe we'll see each other again someday."

He looked at me sadly and trotted away.

I sidled up to the corner of the building and looked down the main street. The guy with the bike was nowhere to be seen. I took one more deep breath and, relieved, started on my way home, but a little faster than usual.

I'd only gone a few steps when I thought suddenly of Ms. Hober-Stratman.

Why couldn't I get her out of my head? I saw her in front of me, the way she went past me in the classroom in her high heels. Then I had an awful thought. The woman in the red dress! Was it Ms. Hober-Stratman I'd seen across the street with the man?

But Ms. Hober-Stratman has black hair . . . but

25

maybe she was wearing a wig, I thought right away. Now my head really was beginning to spin.

If I told Collin about this, he'd be sure he scented a criminal case. Maybe Steffi would even change her mind. But should I even tell them at all? They'd probably just say I was crazy and kid me and say that I saw our bio teacher in every woman. But what if Collin's suspicions were right and Ms. Hober-Stratman had gotten the money by committing a crime? Did the man who was with her have anything to do with it? Her friend! Probably some jerky, stuck-up guy who was only using her. He'd looked so unpleasant, even from behind! Why do the coolest women always pick the wrong men? There was only one thought that gave me any comfort: My imagination must have played a trick on me. Surely the woman with the light blond hair was not Ms. Hober-Stratman, but some other woman I'd never see again.

Deep in thought, I didn't pay any attention to what was going on around me. Just before I reached the door of our building, I heard a soft whistling behind me, like an old teakettle.

Home Wanted!

I DIDN'T HAVE TO TURN AROUND to know who it was, but I did. There he stood, his head cocked, whistling through the gaps in his teeth. I cocked my head, too, and we just looked at each other for a while. The little dog didn't move, until I knelt down. Then he slowly came up to me. The longer I looked at that pitiful little guy, the more I liked him. If you looked past the mangy coat, the bitten-off ear, and the gaps in the teeth, he was kind of nice looking. He only needed a little T.L.C.

"Now then, dude, why are you following me?" I asked him. "And what's your name, anyway?"

I suddenly became aware that I was kneeling in front of a dog in the middle of the street, asking him questions. I looked around, hoping no one had heard me.

I thought about what his name might be: Waldo? Jake? Prince? Fido? Nothing seemed to fit. Anyway, I decided, it would be better not to give him any name at all. I wouldn't be allowed to keep him.

"You can't stay with me, dude," I said to him then. "My mother will never let me have you."

I gave him another little tap. "So go on now, beat it."

Either he didn't understand me, or he didn't want to understand me. Instead of running away he sat down in front of me on the pavement and cocked his head a little more. The whistling had stopped. I guess my voice had calmed him. I already felt a little responsible for him. Compared to him, I had it really good, but I knew if I knelt there in front of him any longer, I'd never have the heart to send him away. So I decided to put an end to it quickly and painlessly. I jumped up without warning and ran up to the door of our apartment building. Luckily, it wasn't far.

I didn't look around, but I was certain he would run after me. I dug into my pocket for the key as I ran and was at the door with one leap. But I wasn't fast enough. Before I could get the key into the lock, the dog jumped up on me, wagging his tail. His tongue was hanging about two feet out of his mouth, and he probably thought I wanted to play with him. That was bad. I'd have to use harsher methods.

"I just told you to beat it!" I yelled at him. "Now get out of here!"

Instantly he leaped off me, backed up three steps, tucked his tail between his legs, and looked at me with big, sad eyes. I turned around, unlocked the door, rushed in, and let the door slam behind me. It almost broke my heart, but I had no other choice. I leaned against the door, exhausted.

All at once there was such a racket outside that I thought my eardrums would explode. How could such a little dog howl like that? I stuck my fingers in my ears, but it didn't help. Finally I couldn't stand it anymore, so I opened the door a crack. Before I knew it, he'd slipped through into the hallway. He stood there whistling triumphantly—I think he was even smiling.

What could I do? I couldn't get rid of him. Then I thought of what my mom had said to me one time when I asked if I could get a dog: "Norbert, I really don't have time to take care of a dog. After all, we live alone, and I can barely manage as it is. Sorry, sweetie."

Even though I promised to take care of him, it didn't do any good. I was really mad about it at the time. And now that I thought about it again, I was even madder! If I couldn't invite my friends home to my house, then I at least wanted to have a dog!

I picked the little whistler up. "I'm going to keep you," I whispered into his mangled ear. "I don't care what Mom says." As if he'd understood me, he cuddled up to me and stopped whistling right away. I had a new friend.

While I was carrying him upstairs to our apartment, I got an amazing idea. He would be a topnotch mascot for Collin and Co.!

I left him in my room while I raided the refrigerator, mixed a bunch of leftovers together, and put it all into a small bowl. It didn't look very appetizing, but my new friend pitched into it as if it were the most delicious thing he'd ever tasted. While he gobbled it down, smacking and grunting, I thought about what I should call him. If he was going to stay with me, then he really did have to have a name, but I still couldn't think of anything that fitted him.

After he'd finished the food, I warmed up my own meal that Mom had left me. My new friend watched me with interest, wagging his tail expectantly. I figured I ought to begin training him right away.

I threw a piece of hamburger at his feet and said severely, "You may only eat that if you promise not to beg again!"

He looked at me guiltily and gobbled it up.

After supper I tried to teach him a few of the simpler tricks. That would certainly convince Collin and the others that we could use him. I began with "Stay" and "Heel." But I got the feeling he didn't understand what I wanted from him, because he just looked at me, cocked his head, and wagged his tail. Sometimes he also whistled softly. I began to wonder if he was a bit dense, but I quickly dismissed the thought.

I looked at the clock. Mom would be home soon, and I wanted to be asleep before then so she couldn't ask me any questions that might possibly make me give myself away. Before I got into bed, I had a long talk with the dog about how important it was that he stay under the bed. I didn't want Mom to see him when she looked in my room later. My mother has eagle eyes whenever there's anything amiss, and it wouldn't take eagle eyes to see a dog hiding in a bedroom.

I'd barely pulled the covers up and I was asleep.

I dreamed about the first big case of Collin and Co. Our assignment was to find the abducted daughter of a millionaire. This daughter was really beautiful—in many ways she resembled Ms. Hober-Stratman, except that she had light blond hair. The dream was very realistic. Collin, Steffi, Radish, and

I were the stars of the dream, but this time I was boss and Collin had to do everything I told him to. It was a great dream. After a wild chase, we'd cornered the gangsters and rescued Ms. Hober-Stratman—I mean the millionaire's daughter. I saw the gratitude in her eyes. We took her to a safe hiding place so she could rest before the people from the newspapers and television began pestering her. But the gangster boss wouldn't give up. He waited for us at night, in a dark side street, along with his bodyguards. Strangely, they all had huge ears and faces full of pimples. Collin ran away, crying for his mom, and Steffi and Radish took off, too, leaving me to take on the crooks alone. After I'd sent three of them to dreamland with a few well-aimed karate chops, the others fell on me. I did everything in my power to defend myself. Four of them had to hold me down while the boss tried to get Ms. Hober-Stratman's— I mean the millionaire's daughter's—hiding place out of me. But I didn't give in. Even when they began to torture me by slapping my face with a wet cloth, I said nothing. The crooks kept hauling off, the cloth sailing through the air whistling. Each time it landed on my face with a loud smack. It was sticky and smelled awful. I tried to get free, but the four bodyguards held me fast with their iron fists.

The first thing I saw when I woke up was a wet

red cloth running up and over my face. Then I heard whistling. I wanted to get up, but I couldn't move. Something was holding my arms. Gradually my eyes got used to the dark and I could see what was going on. The dog was standing over me with his front feet on my upper arms. He was licking my face with his disgusting, slobbery tongue and whistling between licks.

"Dude! Get off, you stinker!" Right away he jumped off my bed.

I wiped my face dry with my pajama top. The smell of dog slobber made me feel sick. I peered through the darkness. The dog was standing by the door whistling and scratching at it like mad. It was instantly clear to me what that meant. He had to go out!

Just what I needed. If he couldn't relieve himself on a tree or a streetlight pretty soon, he would make a puddle on my rug. Then I might as well have just laid him in Mom's bed right then and there.

There was nothing left for me to do but take him out, even if we had to pass Mom's room. Maybe I'd be lucky and she wouldn't wake up.

"Okay I'll take you out. But just be quiet!" I whispered urgently. "If Mom wakes up, we'll both be on the street. And you can sleep in the garbage cans again."

He looked at me as if he'd understood, and unfortunately, I trusted him. But just as we were passing Mom's bedroom door, he began to bark.

Now, of all times! My blood froze in my veins as Mom tore open the door—it was as if she'd been waiting for us to walk by.

"Norbert!" she yelled. "What are you doing up so late?"

"I—uh—I don't know," I answered, my brain flying in fifty directions at once.

At that moment, she saw the dog.

"What's that?" she yelled at me.

"Nothing, Mom. Only a dog."

"Only a dog? Norbert! How often have I told you that you may not have a dog!"

"But, Mom! He ran after me. I tried to get rid of him. And then he howled like mad. Honest! What was I supposed to do?"

"And now what? You know you can't keep him?"

"I don't know, Mom," I replied. I really hadn't thought about what I was going to do.

"Don't know! Don't know!" Mom snorted. "Norbert! Can you at least tell me where you were going in the middle of the night?"

"He has to go out." I looked down. My little friend looked as if he wouldn't be able to hold out much longer.

"Oh, all I need is for him to piddle on the carpet!" Mom cried.

"I'll just go outside with him fast!"

But she held me firmly by the arm. "No way! You are not running around outside at this time of night! I'll go!"

Before I knew it, she'd pulled on her bathrobe, run to the door, and opened it. The dog hadn't grasped what was happening, so he just stood there, wagging his tail at me.

"Now what is it?" Mom called to him. "Are you coming or do I have to carry you?"

He got it. He shot out the door like a streak of lighting.

I didn't have a good feeling as I looked after the two of them.

Even though I was wide awake, I got back into bed. Of course, I couldn't sleep. I lay there in the dark, listening for the door. I didn't have to wait long. After a few minutes I heard it open and shut.

I couldn't stand it. Softly I crept out of bed, opened my door a crack, and peeked out. I couldn't believe it—Mom was alone!

I wrenched the door open. "Where's the dog, Mom?"

"I left him outside. The sooner you separate from him, the better. He didn't make any attempt

to run after me. He probably belongs to someone. They'll be glad when they have him back
again."

"But he wasn't wearing a collar!" I cried. "He's
probably homeless! You are so mean, Mom!"

"I am not mean, Norbert. Just be reasonable."

"But I don't want to be reasonable! I want the
dog!"

"Norbert." Mom sighed.

I hate those sighs. They always give me the feeling that she isn't going to take me seriously. She put
her arm around my shoulders. "Come on, we'll go
into the kitchen, and talk about it."

We didn't say a single word while she made us
both cocoa. I just watched her. Even though I was
mad, I was happy to be with her for a few minutes.
We never seem to do that anymore.

"So," Mom said when we had our steaming
cocoa in front of us. "Let's talk rationally about
this."

I immediately blurted out, "I want my dog
back!" As soon as I'd said it, I knew it was a lost
cause—some rational conversation *I* was having.

"My goodness, Norbert! Don't be so stubborn!
In the first place, it isn't your dog. Who knows who
he belongs to! And besides, you know perfectly well
that we can't keep a dog here."

"Because the super won't let us?"

"Yes, that too, but not only that. An animal wouldn't be happy here. We have too little time to care for it. I can't do it, in any case. You know I have too much to do."

I looked into my cocoa. "I know, Mom."

"Do you understand that, dear? Please look at me when I'm talking to you."

I felt the rage rising in me, the way it always did when it became clear to me that Mom and I couldn't have a life like most other people's. "Yes, I understand!" I cried. "As always! I always have to understand! Why don't you try to understand me for a change? How can I help it that Dad walked out?" The moment I said it I felt bad. "Sorry, Mom. I didn't mean . . ."

At first she didn't say anything. She only looked at me as though she was angry and sad at the same time. Then she put her arm around my neck and gave me a kiss on the forehead. "I wish it were different, too, believe me. And I wouldn't have anything against having a dog if I knew that someone could always take care of him."

"But I could—"

I didn't have to finish. Mom was already shaking her head. "And what happens when you're in school and I'm at work? You can't leave a dog alone that long. Especially when you're keeping him in a second-floor apartment."

I gave up. I could have sworn to Mom all night long that I would take good care of the dog, but it wouldn't have done any good.

"He's probably not there anymore anyhow," I said softly. "And you're probably right, too."

"Thank you for being so reasonable, Norbert. And now, go to bed. We both have to get up early tomorrow."

I finished my cocoa, kissed Mom good night, and went to my room. Mom couldn't sleep either. I saw light through the crack under her door for a long time.

Of Bank Robbers,
Teachers, and Dogs

THE NEXT MORNING I was so tired I almost fell asleep while I was brushing my teeth. I decided not to say any more about the dog during breakfast, since I intended to simply forget him. So I was all the more astonished when Mom suddenly brought the subject up again.

"I must say, Norbert, you seem to have very nice friends. And you're always talking about that detective club, so what do you need a dog for?"

I almost choked on my waffles. She really had no clue! "But that's just it, Mom! You need a dog, as a detective, especially. Everyone knows that! To follow scents, to look for clues! A dog is important for that. You just can't solve some cases without a dog."

"Are you working on any cases now?"

I thought about Ms. Hober-Stratman and our

treasure hunt and preferred not to give any details. So all I said was, "Uh, at the moment it doesn't look particularly good."

Mom laughed out loud. "Why don't you try to solve the bank robbery?"

Why won't anyone take us seriously? "What bank robbery?" I asked, rolling my eyes.

"Haven't you heard about it? It was in the paper a few weeks ago. You really should look at the paper more often, Norbert. You're old enough."

Now it rang a bell. Yeah, sure, Collin had even called a conference about it. We'd discussed whether it could be a case for Collin and Co. But Steffi and Radish were against it—Radish, especially, because he said that it would be much too dangerous.

"Oh, right. So what did the paper say?" I asked abstractedly. I hadn't read the article. Collin only told us about it.

"A bank here in the neighborhood was robbed a few weeks ago. Luckily, no one was hurt, but the criminals got away with a lot of money."

"And they haven't been caught yet?"

"Not so far as I know. Anyway, they don't have many clues to go on. They only know that there were several of them and that one was a woman. They were photographed by the automatic camera, of course, but the photos were no good."

"That's right!" I cried. "Now I remember! But they were masked, weren't they?"

"No. If I remember right, the newspaper said they were wearing big, dark sunglasses—and wigs."

This time I really did choke on my breakfast. Wigs, I kept thinking as I coughed and Mom thumped me on the back. Wigs. . . .

When I got down to the street, I could think of nothing else but the bank robbery. It all fit together! Or did it? The woman I had seen was wearing a wig, certainly. . . . No, not necessarily. The woman looked like Ms. Hober-Stratman, and if it really was she, then she must have been wearing a wig. But if it wasn't Ms. Hober-Stratman, then she might not have been wearing a wig at all. I was getting more and more confused, but I couldn't stop thinking.

Where did Ms. Hober-Stratman get the money for the expensive car? And wasn't it just a few weeks ago that she'd started buying expensive clothes? She could have gotten the money from somewhere else, like winning the lottery, or an inheritance, or just by saving, but if she had, it was an awfully weird coincidence. If I told Collin about it, he'd definitely be convinced that she was one of the gangsters. Then he would certainly do everything possible to find her guilty. And Steffi and Radish would surely back him up. They'd probably even go to the police! And then

Ms. Hober-Stratman would be arrested and I'd have to testify against her in court! And if she were not guilty, then she'd be sitting there in prison for no reason and it would be my fault. I'd never be able to look her in the eye again! No, I couldn't let that happen! I decided not to tell the others about the woman with the wig, the bank robbery, and my suspicions. I'd let the police deal with it. After all, they understand more about crime than we do.

I'd walked to the bus stop so many times I could just set my feet on automatic pilot, so I plodded along, daydreaming. I only noticed the dog after I'd been waiting for a minute or two.

"What are you doing here?" I cried so loud that the people who were waiting for the bus with me turned around to look at me in astonishment.

There he was standing in front of me—disheveled, gap-toothed, chewed-eared—and wagging his tail. Once again, I could have sworn he was grinning at me.

It was a sign! I didn't hesitate for a moment. "I'm taking you to school with me."

His tail rotated like a helicopter rotor. He'd understood me! I had no idea, of course, what would happen when I showed up at school with a dog, but I didn't care. We belonged together! I was positive of that now.

The bus driver almost ruined everything for me. "The dog has to pay half fare," he fussed. Why are bus drivers always in such bad moods? Of course, I'd spent the last of my money for those stupid snacks.

"But I don't have any money!"

"Then the animal stays outside!"

"Let the boy on," a voice beside me said suddenly. I looked around. It belonged to a sweet-looking old woman who was sitting in the first row, fishing in her handbag. "I'll pay the dog's fare. Bad enough that people use these poor animals for laboratory experiments, now they have to pay bus fare, too."

I was just about to thank her when she gave me a stern look. "And you should take better care of your dog, my boy. He looks really pitiful."

I murmured a hasty "Thank you very much" and scurried to the farthest corner of the bus before the other passengers got the idea I'd been doing laboratory experiments on him. Fortunately they were much too busy with themselves and their newspapers to take any interest in me. I settled the dog on my lap and tried not to think about Ms. Hober-Stratman. Instead I considered how I could keep the dog even though Mom was against it. I thought and thought, but I couldn't think of a solution. Perhaps the other members of Collin and Co. would have an idea. Naturally, I'd tell them about the dog. What would they say about him? I hoped they'd be as enthusiastic as I was. Maybe we could even train him together to be a sort of detective dog. I looked at him and immediately began to have doubts. He didn't really look like much of a crime solver. In fact, he looked pretty much the opposite. My mood changed. I was no longer excited about showing him to Collin, Steffi, and Radish—I was afraid to. In my mind I heard them teasing me. Right then I decided to hide him first and figure out how to prepare them to meet my new friend.

On the way from the bus stop to school he didn't move one step from my side. I think he was feeling on top of the world. Just before I got to school, I went into a little side street with him. There was an empty lot there with high grass and bushes. I took him behind a bush and crouched in front of him.

"Now listen to me," I said quietly to him, hoping he'd understand me. "I have to go to school now and you can't come with me. Wait here for me. I'll come get you again afterward. Got it?"

As hard as I tried, I couldn't read anything in his face, so I just had to risk it. I stood up and walked away. I figured he would jump up and run after me, but to my surprise he stayed where he was. I looked around at him once. He was sitting down and looking after me with his head on one side. I desperately hoped he'd still be sitting there when I came back.

When I got to the schoolyard, I was greeted by the usual pushing and shoving. It didn't take long to find Collin, Steffi, and Radish. As usual, they were standing in a corner with their heads together.

"Hi, Norbert," Steffi greeted me. "You're late today. You're usually the first one here. Did you miss your bus?"

I shook my head. Although I was afraid they might not like my dog, I was dying to tell them about him.

"What's the matter with you?" asked Collin. "You look weird."

Steffi laughed. "He looks like that all the time!"

"Dude! Very funny!" I made a face at her as if I was mad. She smiled back at me—I guessed she'd changed her mind about being in the gang. Man, girls can be weird, sometimes.

"So, what's up?" Collin asked once more.

I couldn't hold out any longer. "Actually, some-thing did happen."

All ears pricked up. "What happened?" asked Radish. "Tell!"

"I found a dog. Dude, a really awesome dog. He isn't so gorgeous, but he's really smart."

"A dog!" Collin groaned.

"Yes, a dog! You know how badly I've always wanted one and now I've got one!"

"Okay. Okay. Fine," said Collin. "Pull yourself together. Where is he, then, your superdog?"

"Dude! If you act like that, I won't show him to you at all."

"Okay. All right, where is he?"

"He's waiting for me a block away."

Steffi looked at me with disbelief. "How do you know he's waiting for you?"

"Because I told him to."

"What?" Collin laughed. "Because you told him to? Are you kidding?"

"Nope. I'll show him to you during break. You'll see!"

"But we're not allowed to leave the schoolyard during break," Radish pointed out.

Just then the bell rang for first period.

"Your brother is always so scared," Collin whispered to Steffi as we walked across the schoolyard.

Steffi shrugged her shoulders. "He's always been that way, but when it comes right down to it, you can rely on him."

I have to admit that during the first two periods I didn't really pay much attention to the lessons because now I actually had three problems. I was worried about what Collin and Co. would say about my dog, worried about whether or not he was still waiting for me, and as much as I tried, I could not get Ms. Hober-Stratman and the bank robbery out of my head. We had bio fourth period. How could I look her in the eye?

Our expedition during break went better than expected. Big Al, our English teacher, had proctor duty. So we bribed Kai and Tommy from our class with soda and chocolate bars to stage a fight. That kept Big Al distracted long enough for us to get away without his noticing.

When we turned into the side street where the vacant lot was, my hands got damp and a strange feeling was spreading through my gut. I prayed he would still be there, but I was startled when suddenly he came shooting out from behind a bush, jumping around like mad, trying to lick my face.

"Yuck!" cried Radish. "He's licking you right in the face! Gross!"

For the first time the dog seemed to notice that I wasn't alone. He stopped and stood there, rooted, looking anxiously up at my detective partners. As they regarded my new friend calmly, I tried to read their thoughts in their faces.

47

"Somehow he fits you, Norbert," said Steffi finally. I don't know to this day what she meant by that. But at least she didn't start teasing me about him right off.

"Well, what do you think?" I asked when Collin and Radish didn't say anything.

Collin puffed out his cheeks and blew the air out. "Well, what can I say? He sure is . . . somehow something out of the ordinary."

"Yes, isn't he? That's exactly what I think, too!"

"Why's he missing an ear?" Radish wanted to know.

I shrugged. "Probably lost it in a fight. Besides, he's only missing half."

"In a fight?" asked Steffi, giggling. "Man, I'd sure hate the see the other guy."

Of course, he *had* to show his teeth right as that moment. . . .

"I don't know, Stef. I think the other guy did all right!" Collin roared.

And as if that wasn't enough, he let them hear his gap-tooth whistle.

They convulsed with laughter, clapping each other on the shoulder and hopping around like mental patients, while the object of their laughter jumped around with them, having a good time and whistling even louder. Every time they'd start to calm down again, there'd come a whistle and they'd start all over again.

They finally settled down, but it was probably just because they were so exhausted they couldn't laugh anymore.

Collin wiped the tears from his eyes. "Man, that was totally funny. That dog is really cool."

"And so musical!" cackled Radish.

"Okay, guys, be serious for a minute," said Steffi. "What are you going to do with the dog, Norbert?"

"I think we should keep him."

"We? What do you mean we?" Collin wanted to know.

"I mean Collin and Co., of course. A dog like this could be very useful in solving cases."

Steffi looked pityingly at my little friend. "You know, he really doesn't look the way I'd imagine a detective dog looking, but somehow he's sweet anyway."

Collin put on a disapproving face. "Sweet! What we need is a real detective dog."

"So you agree!" I cried. If Collin was for it, the others wouldn't have anything against it. That's always the way it is in Collin and Co.

"What can he do?" Collin asked.

"He obeys me."

"Okay. That's a beginning. An obedient dog is

also trainable. I say we take him on probation, as a half member, so to speak. Then he can show us what he's got."

I held out my hand to Collin. "Agreed."

He took it.

I looked at the other two. They nodded.

"What's his name, anyway?" asked Steffi.

I shrugged my shoulders. "I can't think of a name that fits him."

"He should have a beautiful name," said Radish. "Then at least he'd have *something* beautiful."

Steffi grinned to her ear lobes. "How about Gorgeous?"

I wanted to protest, but Collin jumped in before I had a chance. "Brilliant, Steffi!" he roared. "That's the gag of the century! We'll call him Gorgeous."

There probably couldn't be a sillier name for a male dog. Nevertheless, I agreed. I was glad that he was accepted by Collin and Co. at all—even as a half member. There was still one problem left.

"We still have to figure out who he can live with," I said softly.

Collin, Steffi, and Radish looked at me, uncomprehending.

"How come?" Radish asked. "I thought he could live with you."

"Unfortunately that won't work. My mother

said no way. I tried everything, but she just won't hear of it. Couldn't one of you—"

"Never!" Steffi interrupted.

"But why not?" said her brother. "There'd be room in our yard."

Steffi tapped her forehead. "Do you have all the cups in your cupboard, little brother? Sure we have room in the yard, but can you imagine what Dad would do if a dog left his calling card on one of his precious roses?"

She was right. We knew only too well how sensitive Mr. Rademacher was when it came to his yard.

"Wait a minute," said Collin suddenly. "I just had an idea. My aunt and uncle have one of the community gardens right here in the neighborhood. They used to have a dog. He's been dead for ages, but the doghouse is still there."

"And you think they would actually let Gorgeous stay in their garden?" Radish asked skeptically.

"I don't know about forever, but we could certainly leave him there for a few weeks. They're on vacation. They go several times a year, and then my parents have to take care of the garden, which actually means my brother and me. So it would be no problem for us to use their doghouse."

With that it was decided that Gorgeous would be moved to Collin's aunt and uncle's garden right after school. I was so glad about it that I volunteered to provide the food for Gorgeous, although I had no idea how I was going to pay for it.

Steffi looked at her watch. "Yikes! If we don't want to get into trouble, we have to hurry."

At almost the same moment the rest of us looked at our watches. She was right, break was over in two minutes.

I knelt before Gorgeous once more and instructed him to stay where he was. Then I ran off after the others toward school. This time I was certain that he would wait for me.

When we got to the schoolyard, the last stragglers were still loitering around, so we still managed to get to class before the teacher.

A Bicycle, a Betrayal, and the Consequences

WE HAD TO WAIT FOR BIG AL AGAIN. He's usually late starting class. Nadine was—as always—seated on the windowsill and was—as always—looking out intently. She did that every teacher-free minute. I wondered what she was looking for. I figure when she's grown up she'll be one of those people who sits at the window all day long, getting involved in all the neighbors' lives.

"Here comes Hober-Stratman!" she shouted so suddenly that all the rest of us were quiet for a moment.

"So?" someone else shouted back. "What's so special about that?"

"She's riding a bike!"

In one leap, half the class was at the window, including me.

Nadine was right. Ms. Hober-Stratman on a bicycle! Not that it was so special to see a teacher on a bicycle. Many of them traveled that way. However, she was wobbling along the street on a bike so ancient it looked as if it would fall apart at any moment.

"She obviously hasn't ridden a bicycle in a while," said Radish.

"Baloney!" said Steffi. "Her dress is too tight. That's why she's riding so funny."

That was true. Ms. Hober-Stratman was looking fantastic again. I'd never seen the dress she was wearing before. It was dark blue—and tight. Much too tight for riding a bicycle. Why would she do such a thing?

"But that isn't the point," said Collin, wrenching me from my thoughts. "Where's the car? First she comes in an old rattletrap, then in a Porsche, and now on a bicycle!"

"You could always ask her," Steffi suggested wickedly.

Collin assumed a defiant expression. "You know what? I will!"

That was a mistake. Immediately Steffi stuck out her hand. "Bet?"

Everyone standing at the window looked at Collin expectantly.

"We have bio the period after next," Steffi persisted. "So, how about it?"

He had no choice. He shook. "Okay, fine. I'll ask her. It's no big deal."

However, his voice trembled a little as he said it. And the rest of us knew why.

Nadine came right over to Collin. "Have fun," she said, smiling pityingly. "You'd better get yourself a bulletproof vest."

During English class I looked over at Collin a few times. Somehow he looked smaller than usual.

After class, I couldn't resist going over to Collin's desk. He gave me a look that I'd never seen on him before—it was a cry for help.

"Do you think she'll finish me off the way she did Nadine the other day?" he whispered.

"Dude! It won't be so bad. Hey, at least she can't hit you. . . ."

"It's all Steffi's fault," he whispered, even more softly. "Why does she always get me to do things I really don't want to do at all."

"Don't forget!" Steffi yelled across the classroom, as if she'd heard what Collin said. "If you don't ask Hober-Stratman, you get to carry my schoolbag for a week!"

"You see?" he whispered to me through the laughter. "That's what I mean." We went to our desks.

Ms. Hober-Stratman walked into the room. "Nice that you're in such a good mood!" her voice boomed through the classroom. "That's the right mood for a little test."

Everyone groaned. Luckily, I'd studied for bio this time. I couldn't forget the humiliation of the last test—besides, I didn't want to let her down again. Since her tests only lasted twenty minutes, it didn't get Collin out of his bet. Nevertheless, he let it go until just before the end of the period.

"May I ask you a question, Ms. Hober-Stratman?" Collin blurted as she was about to explain our homework for the night.

"Certainly, Collin. Was there something you didn't understand?"

"No, that isn't it. It has nothing to do with the lesson, actually."

"Okay. What is it?"

"Uh . . . about your bicycle. That is, actually, I only want to know why you came to school on a bicycle and not in your beautiful new car."

For a long moment it was still. It was as everyone was waiting for the thunderstorm to break. But it didn't happen.

"Well, well," Ms. Hober-Stratman just said softly, and she walked slowly over to Collin's desk. "So you'd like to know something about my bicycle and my car."

"Yes, please, Ms. Hober-Stratman. If it isn't too much trouble."

"Trouble? No, Collin, that isn't any trouble at all—for me." She kept coming closer and closer to him. There was an empty seat near Collin. She sat down, propped her elbows on the desk, put her chin in her hands, and smiled into Collin's face from about four inches away. Why did he always have all the luck?

"Would you like to know anything else, Collin? Perhaps my shoe size or what kind of soap I use?"

"Huh?" Collin's face began to glow bright red.

Ms. Hober-Stratman's smile got wider. "Huh? What do you mean by that, Collin?"

"I only wanted, I mean—uh—really I only wanted to know about the bicycle."

"Okay, Collin. I will tell you why I came on the bicycle: Because I wanted to. And if I feel like it, tomorrow I will come on roller skates and the day after that on a scooter. Do you understand what I am trying to say, Collin?"

Collin gulped. "Yes, ma'am. That I shouldn't be so curious."

She stood up again. "Very good. I'm delighted that you grasped it so quickly." She turned to us. "And that goes for all of you! Concern yourselves with your homework—you all have trouble enough with that."

Then she piled it on. We all thanked Collin on the way out.

I must admit, it was kind of nice seeing Collin enduring all the dumb wisecracks for once. But after a while it got old, so I decided to go off and do some thinking. Just what was wrong with Ms. Hober-Stratman? Her behavior was becoming more and more mysterious. Why *did* she come on a bike today? And why had she gotten so angry just because Collin asked her about the car? Was it perhaps her bad conscience? I was beginning to realize that I couldn't figure it all out alone—I had to tell the others. But then I saw Ms. Hober-Stratman sitting in prison, innocent. What should I do? I ate my snack and thought some more. It didn't help.

By the time the bell rang for the end of school, I'd reached a decision. I would tell Collin, Radish, and Steffi, even if I felt like a traitor doing it!

We'd agreed that we would take Gorgeous to his new home right after school. When he saw us, he jumped all around us, wagging his tail and whistling. Collin scratched his neck absentmindedly. "That dumb teacher!" he growled. "Humiliating me like that!"

"Oh, well," Steffi consoled him, "you won the bet anyway."

"I'd love to know why she acted like that," Radish said. "Collin's question wasn't that bad. Why couldn't she simply say why she came on the bike?"

"She just doesn't want anyone snooping around in her private life."

"But what's snooping around about that?" Collin

was getting worked up again. "Radish is right. That was just a harmless question. A person only reacts like that if she has something to hide."

"Collin might be right." They all looked at me. "I actually have to tell you all something about Ms. Hober-Stratman."

"Really?" Collin cried. "Let's hear it!"

I picked up Gorgeous. "Let's go. I'll tell you on the way."

When I was finished, Gorgeous was lying proudly in his new doghouse in Aunt Peg's community garden.

"Man, is that something!" cried Collin as he dropped onto the old bench in front of the doghouse.

"And do you seriously think that Ms. Hober-Stratman has something to do with the bank robbery?" Steffi asked me.

I shrugged my shoulders.

"But it's more than suspicious, you have to admit," Collin said. "Besides, didn't I say before that we should take an interest in that bank robbery? Oh, man, I didn't cut the article out of the paper. Rats! Did any of you keep it by any chance?"

We all shook our heads.

"What are we going to do now?" Radish wanted to know. "Should we go to the police?"

I was ready for that. "Dude! Why go right to the

police? Shouldn't we snoop around ourselves first?"

Collin nodded. "Norbert is right. We should only involve the police when our suspicions have jelled."

Steffi finally spoke up. "I will admit that it all does sound suspicious. But that doesn't mean that Ms. Hober-Stratman is a bank robber!"

"I can hardly believe it either," Collin agreed. "But it's important that we get to the bottom of this, especially if we know who's involved."

Steffi sighed. "Oh, all right. We can go ahead and try to find out what's wrong with Ms. Hober-Stratman."

Collin jumped up. "Now you're talking! Let's not waste any time. As a matter of fact, I've already thought of something."

"What?"

"Today's Tuesday, right?"

"Yes. So?"

"She always has the bio work group on Tuesday afternoons. I know that from a kid in the class ahead of us. If I'm not mistaken, the class lasts until about three-thirty in the afternoon. Let's meet here at around three o'clock, then we'll go to school and observe her."

I didn't feel too good about this, but I only had myself to blame. I shouldn't have betrayed Ms. Hober-Stratman.

I said a brief good-bye to Gorgeous—promising to bring him a treat later—and headed home.

I was lucky. Lunch wasn't quite ready when I got there. I set the table and sat down, still feeling guilty.

When we were sitting with our plates in front of us, there came the usual question: "How did school go today, Norbert?"

I was about to give her the usual answer, "Fine," when I had an idea. After all, Mom was a woman, too. Maybe she had an idea why Ms. Hober-Stratman had been acting so strangely recently. Maybe there was a perfectly normal explanation.

"Collin had trouble with a teacher today."

"Really? What about?"

"He didn't really do anything bad. It was our bio teacher. She's been acting so funny lately."

I told her about the expensive clothes and the sports car and about how she overreacted if anyone asked about her private life. Of course, I didn't say anything about my suspicions about the bank robbery.

"And today she came to school on a bicycle," I reported. "When Collin asked her about it, she humiliated him in front of the whole class!"

"Maybe her nerves are just a little frazzled. I imagine kids your age could sometimes drive a teacher right up the wall."

"Yeah, I guess," I agreed. "But it's different with her.

The other day Nadine just asked her if she was married, and you should have heard how angry she got."

"So is she married?"

"She wouldn't say, but I don't think so. Do you think that may have something to do with why she's suddenly dressing differently and driving around in a sportscar?"

Suddenly Mom smiled. "Sure. Sounds to me as though she's in love."

I got hot all over. I hoped she couldn't see how embarrassed I was. "What do you mean?"

"Could be that her boyfriend likes beautiful clothes and sports cars. Or that he gave them to her. When people are in love, they do a lot of things that maybe they wouldn't do otherwise."

"So why is she so touchy?"

"Maybe she doesn't want to talk about her personal life because she doesn't want anyone poking around in it."

When Mom said that I realized how little I knew of Ms. Hober-Stratman. She never talked about her family or her home, the way other teachers sometimes did. Did she have a boyfriend or was she married? Or did she have another secret—a bad one?

I wanted to talk to Mom some more about it, but I had to go. Gorgeous was probably starving, and I had to meet Collin and Co. The problem was, how was I supposed to get something edible for Gorgeous? I couldn't raid the refrigerator, because I couldn't get at it without being seen, plus Mom would notice if something was missing. So I put on my best pathetic face.

"Mom?"

"Yes, Norbert?"

"I'm broke."

"Already? We still have half the month ahead of us! Can't you budget your money a little better? I have to do it too, you know."

"Yes, I know. But I had so many expenses this month." I thought of having to spend the last of my money for those stupid snacks and my stomach knotted with rage.

"Advance?" she said with a sigh.

"Thanks, Mom? You're the best!"

As she got her purse out and dug around in it, I started to feel guilty. I know that she has to figure for every penny, and I was probably messing up her house- hold accounts with my advance. But then she smiled and handed me the money, and I felt a little better.

"But it will be deducted next month. You can count on that!"

"Of course!" I cried, but I was almost out the door already. If I wanted to get to Gorgeous before the others, I really had to hurry.

On the way I stopped at the butcher shop to see if they had any leftover odds and ends. I was lucky. When I told the woman behind the counter that it was for my dog, I didn't have to pay anything. My dog! I couldn't believe I had a dog! It was cool!

Gorgeous was sitting proudly in front of his doghouse as if he were guarding it. When he saw me and smelled what I'd brought for him, he went crazy. He jumped around me, wagging his tail like mad. I thought he wouldn't be able to eat, out of pure joy. But when I put the meat down, he gobbled it in one bite.

Just then, Steffi and Radish walked up. "Yuck! What's that?" Steffi squealed when she saw what Gorgeous was wolfing down.

"Dude! What do you mean, yuck? That's perfectly normal sausage. Dogs love it."

"That's obvious," said Radish with a grin.

"But it's not good for them."

"Oh, no? What *should* I give him?" I wanted to know. "Soup and salad?"

"How about dog food, wise guy?"

I rubbed my thumb and forefinger together. "Hey, if you'll pay for it, I'll get him whatever you say. But for now, I'm responsible for his food."

"I know you're feeding him, but he's my business too. After all, he belongs to all of us."

Just then, our boss arrived and jumped right in.

"Sure, the dog has to get something decent down his throat. After all, he has to be fit for training."

"Dude! What training?"

"Man, we've already discussed that! He supposed to help us with our work. And to do that he must, of course, be trained."

"What's he supposed to do?" Steffi asked. She was looking as if she were about to burst out laughing.

"You know, pick up scents and stuff." Collin looked around. He picked up an old branch from the ground, knelt down, and stretched the branch out in front of him.

"Gorgeous!" he cried. "Look what I have here!"

Gorgeous pricked up his ears and looked at Collin.

"Come on, Gorgeous! Jump over the sticky!"

Gorgeous ran over to Collin and his "sticky." Unfortunately, instead of jumping over the branch, he grabbed it in his teeth and ran away.

"Hey! Stop, you dummy!" Collin bellowed after him. But it didn't do any good. Like lightning, Gorgeous raced across the garden with his new plaything and right out of the open gate to the street.

"Man, he's running toward school!" cried Radish. "We've got to catch him before Ms. Hober-Stratman comes!"

Walking in Pursuit

RADISH WAS RIGHT. There was only a small park between the school and the community gardens. Gorgeous headed straight for the schoolyard. As luck would have it, just before we caught up with him there, kids started piling out of the doors. Luckily Ms. Hober-Stratman wasn't there yet.

"Stop the dog!" Collin yelled, but Gorgeous was past them before they had any idea what was happening. More and more kids were streaming out into the schoolyard. Finally, one of them noticed Gorgeous. He knelt down in front of him and spread out his arms. As if on cue, Gorgeous jumped up at him, laid the stick on his knee, and licked his face from top to bottom. I have to admit that I was jealous. I would have been so proud if he'd done it to me, but no—he did it to a total stranger!

"Is that your mangy old mutt?" called a mean-looking kid I'd seen around school. "He looks just like a barking toilet brush!"

I ran to Gorgeous and picked him up. "Dude! In the first place he's not mangy, and in the second place, if I were you, I'd take a look in the mirror before I made remarks like that."

I'd certainly have argued with that idiot longer if Collin hadn't grabbed my jacket and pulled me with him. He dragged me into a niche behind the main door. Shortly afterward, Steffi and Radish were with us. We pressed close together with our backs to the wall. I was still holding Gorgeous in my arms. He was having a blast. He wagged his tail non-stop and kept slapping me in the face with it.

"Big help, your dog," Steffi hissed at me.

"Oh, so now suddenly it's my dog?" I shot back at her.

Then Collin rammed his elbow into my side so hard that I thought he'd broken a few of my ribs. "Shut up! Okay, Hober-Stratman has her bike today. How are we going to follow her?"

Radish waved that away. "The way she's riding in her tight dress, we could probably keep up with her walking and drinking coffee at the same time."

Shortly thereafter, Ms. Hober-Stratman came out to the schoolyard and got her bicycle. Close up it looked even more dilapidated. She didn't see us, and the guys from the bio work group didn't give us away either. A few of them looked over at us, but apparently they didn't connect our strange behavior with Ms. Hober-Stratman.

It took a while for her to get on and get going. Then she rode precariously away. She was going so slowly that it really wasn't a problem to follow her. Plus, every time she'd come to a red light, instead of stopping there and staying seated with one foot on the ground, she'd jump off the bike with such strange contortions that once she almost fell.

I held Gorgeous in my arms while we were following her. That was a pain, of course, and earned me harsh looks from Steffi, but I didn't want to risk his running away from us again.

Completely unexpectedly, Ms. Hober-Stratman jumped off her bike in front of an old apartment house.

We quickly hid ourselves inside a gateway and looked carefully around the corner.

"Does she really live there?" Radish asked.

"Looks like it," Collin answered. "Although the building doesn't exactly look as though people who can afford expensive cars live there."

He was right. The house looked a lot like the one

where we live—and I've already said what I think about that place.

"She's opening the front door!" cried Collin so loud that I was afraid Ms. Hober-Stratman would hear him. But she disappeared inside the building with her bicycle without turning around.

It was only then that I noticed I was still carrying Gorgeous. I set him down, panting, on the ground.

"It will be hilarious," Steffi needled, "if we have to carry our great detective dog every time we run in pursuit of someone. Hey, why don't we just put him in a baby carriage?"

"Hey, man! We weren't running in pursuit, we were walking in pursuit. And if you don't like it, you can bring Gorgeous back all by yourself the next time he runs away from us."

"Guys, can we get back to the subject here?" Radish intervened. "Just look at what a broken-down hovel Ms. Hober-Stratman lives in!"

"We noticed, Brother dear. Do you think we should get her a new one?"

Collin looked around angrily. "You're all missing the point here! Something isn't right. First she has a fantastic car and expensive clothes, then suddenly she's on a broken-down bike and lives in a kennel!"

I didn't say anything. But I thought it would be a

good idea not to invite them home to my house any-time soon.

"So what are we going to do now?" asked Radish.

Collin shrugged his shoulders. "The only thing we can do at the moment is wait, observe the build-ing, and hope we find out something."

I, of course, did not have the faintest idea what we were supposed to find out if we stood in a door-way and observed the building, but I didn't have a better idea, so I didn't say anything.

"How do we know she lives there?" Radish asked when we'd been standing there for quite a while. "I don't think this place goes with her at all."

"Man, Radish!" cried Collin. "You're right. Maybe it's not her apartment at all!"

"Dude! She had a key."

"That doesn't mean anything. Could be that it's her friend's apartment, or a relative's. My parents have the key to my grandma's apartment."

"Maybe Ms. Hober-Stratman is taking care of her old grandmother," Radish offered.

Our boss shook his head. "I thought of some-thing else."

"What?"

"Accomplices! She's meeting there with her accomplices from the bank robbery. I was thinking about the bank robbery some more today. It wasn't far from here. Maybe the bank robbers rented this apartment so they wouldn't have too long an escape route."

"And now they're meeting in the apartment and dividing up their loot?" Steffi asked skeptically.

"It could be!"

"Baloney!"

"It's not baloney at all! Safe house. You hear that all the time!"

"Now, let's just wait and see what happens!" said Radish, trying to calm the squabblers. "We can't do anything else at the moment anyhow."

He was right. So we waited. And again the thoughts were whirling around in my head. If Ms. Hober-Stratman really did have something to do with the bank robbery, she would have to go to prison. Then who could say if I would ever see her again.

At first nothing happened at all. Sometimes on TV you see private detectives or police watching suspects' houses. Now I was finding out for the first time what that really meant. It's probably the most boring thing to do ever! You want something to happen so badly, that you see something suspicious behind every little thing.

We hid there for what seemed like hours. Steffi kept yammering that she wanted to go home. Out of sheer boredom she even played with Gorgeous, although he kept licking her and every time he did, she'd get mad and push him away again. Collin and Radish kept flipping out whenever anyone even got near the door of Ms. Hober-Stratman's building.

I must have heard "Man, that guy looked really suspicious!" or "We have to look at that one under a magnifying glass!" at least twenty times that afternoon.

But then it really did get exciting. Radish saw him first. "Look at that!" But it hadn't been necessary—we'd noticed him, too. A red sports car was driving slowly up the street.

"Dude! That's—"

"Ms. Hober-Stratman's new car!" Radish finished.

We observed the car with bated breath. It drove slowly, almost at walking speed, as if the driver were looking for something. Then he finally stopped near the house Ms. Hober-Stratman had gone into.

A man got out. You could see even from a distance how expensive his suit was, but that wasn't all. It was the way he walked, carried himself, looked around disapprovingly at the houses: he definitely didn't belong in this neighborhood.

Collin poked me. "Is that the guy you saw on the street? The one who was with the blond woman?"

I shook my head immediately. "No, that guy looked completely different. Not so spiffed up, more ordinary."

"Ordinary, huh? I can do a whole lot with that."

"Shut up for a minute!" Steffi hissed at us. "I want to know where the guy is going."

At first it looked as though he had nothing to do with Ms. Hober-Stratman, because he walked right past the door to her building. But then, abruptly, he turned around, looked uncertain for a moment, then walked back and pushed one of the buttons on the door. A moment later, the door opened and he went in.

"Dude! I bet he's going to see Ms. Hober-Stratman!"

"Sure! Where else? I just said she has accomplices!"

At that moment, the man in the expensive suit came back out of the building. He went to the sportscar, bent over, looked inside briefly—and walked on!

"Dude! He just left the car there!"

"Now I'm really confused!" cried Collin. "Come on! After him!"

"What about Ms. Hober-Stratman?"

Collin waved his hand dismissively. "We can always observe her. After all, we see her in school every day. But we might never have another opportunity to shadow her accomplice again."

It was turning out as I'd feared: Collin was convinced Ms. Hober-Stratman was a bank robber.

He was in his element. "Norbert, you carry Gorgeous again, just in case."

I was about to protest, but Collin was already off and away. There was nothing else for me to do than to carry my little friend again. He didn't resist...actually, I had the feeling he kind of liked it.

Ms. Hober-Stratman's accomplice—as Collin kept calling him—wasn't in a hurry. He sauntered along the street as if he had nothing better to do. It was a long chase. The neighborhood he finally led us to looked entirely different from the one where Ms. Hober-Stratman lived.

"Does he live here? Only people with dough live here," Steffi said.

"Nothing surprises me anymore," I said.

He stopped in front of one of those big gates where you'd expect to find a vicious dog or at least an alarm system, pulled out a key, opened it, and vanished inside.

The gate was massive and made of wrought iron, with a wall to the left and right of it at least six feet high, blocking the view. We could only see through a tiny crack between the gates, but it was obvious that the house that went with the entrance had cost a great deal of money.

We were so busy trying to get a view of the house that we got careless.

"What are you doing there?" a voice suddenly said behind us.

My heart slipped to my knees. We all wheeled around simultaneously. The woman standing in front of us looked like the kind you see in Hollywood or in fashion magazines.

"We . . . uh . . . we only wanted to look a little," was our answer—very intelligent.

"Well, now you have. Now get out of here."

She shoved us aside and pressed the button of the call box at the side. "Yes?" crackled out of the speaker. "It's me, darling!" she answered.

At the sound of a soft buzzing, the gates sprang open, and the supermodel quickly vanished behind them.

"Stuck-up cow!" Steffi hurled after her.

"Did you hear that?" cried Collin.

"What?" I asked.

"She called him 'darling.' First he meets with Ms. Hober-Stratman, and then another one calls him darling. Very suspicious!"

"What's so suspicious about it?" Steffi asked.

"That means that Ms. Hober-Stratman isn't his friend and can only be his accomplice. It's perfectly logical!"

I didn't think it was logical at all. Of course, it would have been perfectly fine with me, if this guy weren't Ms. Hober-Stratman's friend, but it didn't make me feel any better to have him be her accomplice.

"Do you think she'll come out again soon?" asked Radish.

I looked at my watch. "Dude! It's so late! Let's just go home. Now that we know where he lives, we can come back again later if we think of something else."

I turned around and was just about to leave when Steffi grabbed me by the arm. "Look there! See what it says on the nameplate?"

I looked. Engraved there in big, black letters was the name: HOBER.

I was so confused that I still carried Gorgeous in my arms for most of the way home, although it wasn't necessary anymore. At that point I didn't really care if he ran away or not.

"The whole thing is getting more and more mysterious," said Collin. "This guy has almost the same name as Ms. Hober-Stratman."

"Are they related to each other?" Radish said, more to himself than to the rest of us.

"What do you mean, related?" his sister asked. "They're married!"

I thought I wasn't hearing right. "Dude! What about his girlfriend? You just saw her yourself."

"Haven't you ever heard of people still having a girlfriend even if they're married?"

Collin nodded importantly. "That happens a lot in gangsterland."

That was too much for me. "That is not true! No way!" I cried, really upset now. "We'd certainly know if Ms. Hober-Stratman were married. And she certainly has nothing to do with gangsters. Besides, his name is Hober, not Hober-Stratman."

Steffi puffed out her cheeks and blew out a frustrated breath. "Man, Norbert! Are you living on the dark side of the moon? These days it's perfectly normal for women to keep their maiden names, even when they're married. And some also use a double name. She used to be named Stratman and now she's married and so she's named Hober-Stratman."

I couldn't believe it!

Collin grinned at Steffi and clapped me on the shoulder. "Take it easy, pal. You have to look truth in the face, even if you are in love."

I was suddenly tired. I had no strength to argue with him anymore. Besides, that would only lead to more teasing about my feelings for Ms. Hober-Stratman. They had no idea what I was going through.

"It's already late," was all I said. "Let's go home."

Collin decided to postpone our investigation until the next day. He assigned us all the task of thinking about the Hober-Stratman case so we could find out as quickly as possible what our teacher and her "friend" were up to. At that moment I wished I'd never said a thing about it.

Dinner with Mom passed without incident, and I fell asleep almost as soon as I got into bed.

When I woke up the next morning and realized that I hadn't dreamed, I was really glad. I hurried to get out of the house—since I'd started feeding Gorgeous, time in the mornings had become very short.

This time, I had less luck at the butcher's than the day before. Another saleslady waited on me and she let me pay for the sausage ends I asked for.

An even worse disappointment awaited me when I got to Gorgeous: He wouldn't touch his food. I hoped he wasn't sick! Since I was pressed for time, I left the expensive, paid-for cold cuts outside his house and made tracks for school. Perhaps he just didn't want anyone to watch him eating this morning.

When I entered the schoolyard, Collin, Steffi, and Radish were already huddled together. Collin was delivering a long lecture. I didn't have to hear it to know what it was about.

". . . so it's decided that that's how we'll proceed," he was saying.

"Dude! What's decided?"

"Collin thought we should go to the villa again this afternoon and try to find out more about this Hober guy."

"Oh, that's very interesting! And why was something like that decided when I wasn't here? Don't I have a say anymore?"

"You see!" cried Radish. "I told you we should wait for Norbert."

"How can I help it if he comes so late."

"Dude! I had to feed Gorgeous, remember? Or do you want to do it from now on?"

Collin gave me a strange look. "That isn't a bad idea at all. Anyway, I think we should concern ourselves more with his training instead of constantly carrying him everyhere! So, people, we'll meet at four o'clock at Gorgeous's, as agreed."

I didn't believe my ears. "Why so late?"

"I have some stuff to do," was all Collin replied, and he turned away, because the bell had rung for first period.

Four o'clock! We'd never yet met so late. Either Collin had lost his marbles, or . . . suddenly I had a suspicion.

It was almost three o'clock when I finally finished my homework after school. I had to hurry, because I wanted to be sure to get to Gorgeous before the others. That was the only way I could find out whether what I suspected of Collin was true.

I was anxious about what I'd find as I set out for Gorgeous's place. When I came to the entrance to the community gardens, I stopped and looked carefully over the hedge. I knew it! Collin was with my dog! It took a while before I grasped what the two of them were really doing there. Collin was teaching Gorgeous tricks—at least, he was trying to. First he let Gorgeous sniff at a little stick and then he threw it. Then Collin looked at Gorgeous and Gorgeous looked at Collin, tongue lolling and tail wagging. Then Collin brought the stick back. He did the whole thing over again two or three more times. Then he tried to get Gorgeous to run along behind him. But as Collin ran around the property, Gorgeous just stood there watching him with interest.

I couldn't stand it anymore. I ran over to the two of them.

"Dude! What's he supposed to be when you're finished?"

"Someone has to train him," Collin panted. "After all, none of you are doing it."

Gorgeous looked as though he were glad that I'd finally rescued him from Collin's "training lessons."

"More likely, he was training you."

Gorgeous's breakfast was still lying where I'd left it that morning.

"Dude! Come clean, have you been feeding him?"

Collin looked at the ground. So it was true!

"What's wrong with you?" I screamed at him. "You know we decided that *I* was going to take care of him. I used my last money to buy food for him, and now he won't eat it because you've already fed him."

He dug his hands into his pants pockets. "Yeah, yeah, I know. Sorry."

"Why'd you do it then?"

He looked at me. I'd never seen him so embarrassed. It was a while before he began to speak. "I just don't think it's fair that you're the only one allowed to feed him."

"Fair?"

"Yes! After all, it's our dog, not just yours, even if you did find him. And I was afraid he'd only obey you if you always bring him the food. Plus, I've always wanted a dog!"

"But you've always just hassled me when I talked about getting a dog!"

Collin scratched around in the sand with one foot. "I know. I only acted as if I couldn't stand dogs because I didn't want to admit that I wanted one too."

"Interesting."

Collin's eyes widened suddenly. "Man, Norbert! Please don't say anything to Steffi about this! It would be total humiliation for me. Okay? I promise that from now on you can feed Gorgeous all by yourself. Just let me play with him now and then."

It was cool! Finally, for once, I felt superior to Collin. He's always the strongest, the one who knows everything, the one in control, and now he was standing there in front of me, a quivering mess. I have to admit I enjoyed it!

I let him twist for a while longer before I let him off the hook. "Okay, Collin. No problem. I won't say anything to Steffi and Radish. But I don't want to provide for Gorgeous all by myself either. We can buy the food together. Then we can get regular dog food and take turns with the feeding. Steffi's already been on my case about what I feed him anyhow."

Collin beamed like a little kid with a new toy. "Norbert, you're the best! I'll never forget this!"

"That's all right," I answered magnanimously. I didn't mention the fact that I really was glad that I didn't have to pay for Gorgeous's food all by myself anymore.

Since it was still early, we played with Gorgeous for a while. It was really fun. I've rarely gotten along so well with Collin. When Steffi and Radish came, they joined in, much to Gorgeous's delight.

"Okay, guys, it's time," Collin grew serious. "Or we won't need to go at all."

"Are you going to carry Gorgeous again?" asked Steffi as we started out.

"Leave Norbert alone!" Collin snarled at her. "He's knows what he's doing with Gorgeous."

And so I experienced my second surprise that afternoon . . . namely, a speechless Steffi!

In order not to get lost, we went to the Hober mansion villa the same way we'd gone the day before. So we also passed the building into which Ms. Hober-Stratman had disappeared.

"Look," cried Radish. "The car's still there in front of the door."

"Dude! Then she *must* live there."

"Not necessarily," Collin replied. "She could also just be visiting. In any case, we should find out about her when we're done with this guy."

Steffi was right about one thing. Collin really did watch too many crime shows.

"I'd love to look at the car up close," Collin went on.

We had no problem with that. Who wouldn't like to look at a sports car?

"Man, look how high the tachometer goes!" marveled Radish as we were standing around the car and pressing our noses against the glass.

"That doesn't mean anything," said Collin expertly. "What's important is how fast she'll *really* go."

I don't know why, but for some reason I turned to look behind me. As I did, I was so startled I almost dropped Gorgeous. I grabbed Steffi by her jacket sleeve and pulled her into the nearest entryway with me.

"Man, Norbert! What's—"

I didn't let her finish. "Shush!" I hissed at her. "Be quiet!" By this time the other two had realized something was happening and were crowding in with us. We pressed against the wall.

"What's the matter, Norbert?" whispered Collin. "You look as if you'd run into Frankenstein."

I felt as if I'd run the marathon. I couldn't catch my breath. "The woman with the wig," I gasped. "She just came out of Ms. Hober-Stratman's house! I hope she didn't see us!"

I'd hardly finished speaking when she walked right past us. We squeezed ourselves tighter against the wall. Luckily, she didn't see us. Still, we recognized her in spite of the blond wig. It was Ms. Hober-Stratman!

The Woman in the Wig

FOR A LONG MOMENT THERE WAS SILENCE. But then Steffi, Radish, and Collin exploded: "Man, that was Hober-Stratman!"

"Why's she wearing such a funny wig?"

"So then you *did* see her, Norbert!"

So I was right. But I'd rather have been wrong. Now it was almost certain: my Ms. Hober-Stratman was a bank robber!

Collin saw it that way too. "Let's go!" he cried. "After her. That's our first real proof!"

We peered cautiously out of the entryway into the street. It was easy to spot her, the blond hair glowed like the sun. We followed her, crisscrossing through the city. Sometimes I had the feeling she was purposely taking roundabout routes, yet she walked purposefully, as though she knew exactly where she was going. She made a brief stop once, bought a newspaper, and stuck it under her arm. Shortly after that she reached her goal. It was a small café in a side street.

"What's she want there?" Radish asked.

"She's probably meeting someone there," his sister said.

"Of course that's what she's doing," said Collin. "People are always meeting each other in cases like this."

Of course I had no idea what he meant by "cases like this," but I, too, would have bet that this little café was a meeting place.

"I'd give anything to be able to go in there after her," Steffi said.

Collin jumped at the idea immediately. "We'll do just that!"

"Are you crazy? What'll you say to her if she asks you what you're doing here?"

"What do you mean? It's not against the law to go into a café, is it?"

"Sure, sure, and then you can ask her why she has on that funny yellow hair," Steffi needled.

He gulped.

"Maybe we could peek through the window," I suggested.

We all agreed on that. We sneaked up to the café. There was only one window beside the entrance, but it reached almost to the ground. When we'd gotten about one step away from the glass, we stopped and pressed ourselves against the wall next to each other.

"Who's going to do it?" our boss asked.

"I am!" I cried and was amazed at myself, but I just had to know who Ms. Hober-Stratman was meeting. Was it the same man I'd already seen her with once, or was it perhaps that Hober, who was possibly her husband? I wondered why I was doing this to myself. She was only my bio teacher, after all. None of it was any of my business, and yet I would have given my eye teeth to know what her secret was. And she had one—that was as certain as the next math test.

"Very good, Norbert," said Collin with relief. "We can always use volunteers."

Without a word, I pressed Gorgeous into his arms. Collin was clearly thrilled about that. With my back pressed against the wall I worked myself inch by inch to the window of the café. Finally, I was standing so that I only had to move my head forward a little in order to be able to see in.

I took a deep breath, looked—and saw nothing. Exactly at that spot there was a large poster with a coffee cup on it stuck to the window. There were a few inches of free window surface underneath. I knelt on the ground and looked through the glass once more. I was lucky this time. Ms. Hober-Stratman had picked out a table near the window and was sitting down so that I could see her face. Fortunately, she was turned away from the window, talking with some man who was sitting opposite her.

So I'd been right. She *was* meeting someone . . . and it was not Mr. Hober. Was it the man I'd seen her with on the street? I strained my eyes so hard that I thought they'd fall out of my head. I could only see him from behind, and I'd also only seen the man on the street from behind. Unfortunately, though, it's very hard to recognize people from behind. He turned around briefly so I could see his face, but I'd never seen him before, I was sure of that. In any case, I didn't like him.

Ms. Hober-Stratman seemed to be thinking something similar. One look at her face was enough to see that she was angry. I know that facial expression well. The last time I'd seen it was when she gave me back my bio test.

Suddenly someone pulled on my jacket. It was Collin. "What's going on, Norbert? Are you going to spend the night there, or what? Do you see her? Is she alone? Is there an accomplice with her?"

I stood up and reported briefly. Now suddenly all

of them wanted to risk a look. One after another they knelt and peered through the window.

"She looks pretty mad," declared Radish, who was the last one.

"You can tell by one look at him that he's a gangster."

"How in the world do you know that?" Steffi asked. "You can't even see his face."

"The way he looks from behind is enough. If we only had some better equipment!"

"What do you mean?"

"Microphones, for instance, that let you hear speech through walls. We sure could use one of those right now!"

"You can just buy one out of your next allowance."

"Ha, ha, ha! Okay, let's go over to the other side of the street. We can observe the café from there."

"Let me look once more," I interrupted them.

I knelt down and looked through the window again. Now I could clearly see that two of them were arguing. Ms. Hober-Stratman was really yelling—I wouldn't have been surprised if we'd heard her outside. And then suddenly she stood up and ran to a door at the other side of the room.

I jumped up so fast that Collin jumped back a step in surprise.

"Dude! She stood up."

"Is she coming out?" cried Collin, getting ready to run.

I held him back. "No, she went out back. There's a door there, too."

"The back entrance! She's going out the back entrance!"

"Baloney!" Steffi declared. "She probably just went to the bathroom."

Collin's eyes brightened. "But there are usually windows there, too. Let's go around to the back. Maybe we can see something."

Steffi frowned. "What's so interesting about a bio teacher going to the bathroom?"

"Who says that's what she's doing?" he cried. "There's probably an exchange of money or something taking place. They always do that in the bathroom."

We couldn't hold him anymore. He was already under way. We had to look for a while before we found a path that led to the back of the building. After we'd climbed over some small walls, we found ourselves standing under the window of the café's bathroom.

"Who's going to look in?" It was the question I'd been waiting for.

"I am!" said Steffi, this time without hesitation.

"That's all we need, for any of you to look in the ladies' room."

As softly as possible we rolled some garbage cans under the window. Steffi climbed up and peered through the half open window.

"She's in there!" she whispered excitedly.

"And?" Collin whispered back. "What's she doing?"

Steffi looked through the window, spellbound, for what seemed like an eternity. Then, she jumped down from the garbage can and stood there looking at us.

"What's the matter?" her brother wanted to know.

"You won't believe it, but she's combing her hair."

"How interesting," remarked Collin, rolling his eyes.

"No! I mean, she was combing her *own* hair! "

"Dude! You mean she took off the wig?"

"Exactly! And not only that, she stuffed it in the trash can!"

"Why'd she do that?"

"How should I know?"

"And you didn't see any money?" Collin asked.

"No!" Steffi snorted. "It's a miracle I could see anything at all."

"Let's go!" cried Collin. "We have to go back before she escapes. Now it's going to get exciting. I just know it!"

We were completely out of breath when we stood at the entrance to the café again.

"Now it's your turn again, Norbert," our boss commanded, although it was unnecessary. I'd already gone to the window.

But when I looked into the café, I knew we wouldn't learn anything more today. Ms. Hober-Stratman and the man she'd been arguing with were gone.

"Dude!"

"Man, Norbert!" hissed Collin. "Not so loud. Do you want them to bust us?"

"They can't. They're gone."

He was beside me in one leap.

"What lousy luck! They can't have gone far. Maybe we can still find them!"

And again we were running along behind our boss. At this rate, I'd be as thin as Radish in no time.

"It's as if they vanished into thin air!" Collin wailed when at last we were standing, gasping, at the corner of a building after a protracted run through the streets around the café.

But then right away he asked, "Have we already looked there?" He was pointing to a narrow street—a street too narrow for even the smallest car.

"I've had it!" cried Steffi. "The only thing left is for us to do is to crawl around in the sewers and look for them."

"She's certainly long gone by now," said Radish.

Collin shook his head. "I don't think so. We checked that way first. She was nowhere to be found."

"Maybe she just had too big a lead. Anyway, I don't think there's any sense in looking anymore."

Collin looked at his watch. "You're right, Radish. It's time to go home, anyway. Still, it annoys me to have lost them. I would just love to know where they are. One of us should have stayed in front of the café as a lookout!"

"It's too late to argue about that now," said Radish. "And how do you know they left together? After all, they had a fight."

"Well, then, we could at least have followed the guy. At the moment, he interests me more than Ms. Hober-Stratman."

"What do you s'pose they were arguing about?" Steffi asked.

"About the loot, probably," was Collin's answer.

"Dude! How do you know that? People can argue about a thousand things!"

"Wearing a wig? Come on, it's clear that Ms. Hober-Stratman didn't want to be recognized. And why wouldn't she want to be recognized? Because the had something to hide! And that something, as we all know, is probably the bank robbery! So the argument had to have been about the bank robbery. Use your brain, Norbert!"

"So then why did she take off the wig and throw it away in the ladies' room?"

"She's probably being blackmailed, too!" Radish suddenly chimed in in the middle of all this.

Collin's eyes widened. "Good, Radish, really good! I didn't think of that. But it's a definite possibility. The guy observed her during the bank robbery and now he's blackmailing her!"

Radish beamed. "Exactly! And today she gave him the money he demanded. That's why she was so angry, too! And then when it was all over, she threw away the wig because then she had nothing more to fear!"

Collin didn't say anything, but he clapped Radish on the shoulder in recognition.

Blackmail! Bank robbery! They were obsessed. And who was giving poor Ms. Hober-Stratman the benefit of the doubt? No one! Sure, it was possible that she was being blackmailed, but still, it could be for other, very different reasons, too. Perhaps she'd made some kind of a mistake once and now had to pay for it for the rest of her life.

"I'm going to run the whole thing through my head once more at home," Collin announced. "We can discuss it first thing in the morning."

We started home. While we walked along beside each other in silence, I had an idea that I couldn't shake. But in order to put it into action, I had to go back to the café once more—alone! I wracked my brain trying to figure out how I could get away from the others without their noticing.

Finally, I had the solution. I stopped. "Dude! I still have to buy fruit! I totally forgot! I promised my mother because she has to work today. So, so long till tomorrow! I'll take Gorgeous to his house later!"

Before the others had time to react at all, I turned and ran off in the opposite direction. It wasn't until two streets further—when I was sure they couldn't see me any longer—that I leaned against the wall of a building to catch my breath.

Gorgeous was whistling softly to himself. He was probably hungry. It served him right. He had been unfaithful to me, too.

"That's what you get. Now you have to wait until I'm finished."

At first I was going to let him walk, but then I felt sorry for him and picked him up again.

What I had in mind could get very embarrassing. The most important thing was for no one in the café to notice me.

But I knew I could forget that hope the minute I closed the door behind me.

"Can I help you?" asked a waitress with a white apron and an order book in her hand.

I looked around for an excuse. Suddenly, Gorgeous let out a whistle and I had it! "My dog is so terribly thirsty!" I wailed. "Can I get him some water in the bathroom?"

The woman looked at Gorgeous pityingly. "The poor fellow. He really does look done in. Wait, I'll get you a dish. The restrooms are back there."

I was about to answer that I knew that, but I caught myself. I walked to the back. I'd hardly found the bathrooms when I faced a second problem. I had to go into the ladies'! If someone caught me doing it, I was done for. I looked around me. None of the patrons were making any motions to stand up. I briefly considered whether there might be someone in the ladies' room at that moment. I had to take the risk! I took a deep breath and went in.

I was lucky—for once. There was no one inside. I discovered what I was looking for immediately. The wig lay half-covered with paper towels in the wastebasket, just as Steffi had said. With one grab I fished it out and stuck it under my jacket.

I hesitated for just a moment longer. Then I pushed open the door and walked out without looking once to the left or right. Then I ran out the door and down the street as fast as I could with Gorgeous in my arms and the wig under my jacket. I only stopped when I was quite certain that no one was following me.

I did it! It had actually worked! Now I had a personal memento of her. Whatever happened, no one would ever get this wig away from me!

The Society for Abused Animals

COLLIN AND I HAD AGREED that the next day he would take over feeding Gorgeous, so I took my time having breakfast. Still, I missed the little guy and was almost sorry I'd "changed shifts" with Collin.

He met us in the schoolyard in a very good mood. He was the first one there—I wondered when he'd gotten up.

"You didn't forget Gorgeous, did you?" I whispered to him when Steffi and Radish couldn't hear.

He gave me an offended look. "What do you take me for?"

Steffi caught that. "We take you for the greatest detective of all time, of course!"

"Someday you'll say that to me and you'll mean it," countered Collin.

"Well, then, why don't you start by telling us your thoughts on yesterday. You certainly didn't go to bed without mulling over the Ms. Hober-Stratman case, did you?"

"Of course not. Only I mulled less than I was annoyed. If we only hadn't lost that guy from the café yesterday . . ."

"I think the best thing would be for us to divide up," I suggested. "One group observes Ms. Hober-Stratman's apartment and the other, the mansion."

"Good plan," Collin said, beaming. "I was just about to suggest it myself. You and Radish, you keep watch on Ms. Hober-Stratman. Steffi and I will cover the house. Keeping suspects under surveillance has always been S.O.P. in solving crimes."

Steffi grinned, but she didn't say anything. I think she saw through Collin ages ago.

But what we all didn't know yet was that Ms. Hober-Stratman herself was going to scrub Collin's beautiful plan.

It began with her giving us a heck of a scare during the next break.

As always, we'd withdrawn to our "conference corner," that is, a remote part of the schoolyard where no one ever goes during the break. You can discuss things there in peace and quiet without someone listening in all the time, or so we thought.

We were arguing about whether Radish and I or Steffi and Collin should take Gorgeous that afternoon when Ms. Hober-Stratman suddenly walked up to us. None of us had heard her coming and we never expected her, since teachers hardly ever come over to that corner.

"You shouldn't just stand around during the break with your heads together," she said sternly. "Some exercise would certainly do you all some good."

"Dude! We didn't have any idea that you were on duty today, Ms. Hober-Stratman," I finally blurted out after we had stared at her in shock for a minute. As soon as I'd said it, I knew how dumb it had sounded.

"Well, now you do know, Norbert. I hope it comforts you."

What had she meant by that? Did she know how I felt?

She turned around and drifted away. If someone had tapped me, I would have fallen over, stiff as a board.

Ms. Hober-Stratman had only gone a few steps when Mr. Barnes appeared. He'd come from the other side, so he couldn't see us. He's our math teacher. We all call him "Handsome Harry," because he looks at himself at least three times during every math period in the little mirror he keeps in his desk drawer—someone found it one day when we had a substitute.

He'd barely caught sight of Ms. Hober-Stratman when he put on a toothpaste-ad smile. "Good morning, my dear colleague," he purred. "All by yourself on the circuit through the wilds of Kurdistan?"

That was probably supposed to be a joke. Ms. Hober-Stratman did not change her expression.

"Shall we walk a ways together?" Handsome Harry tried again.

"No, thank you, Mr. Barnes. I prefer to walk alone."

He placed himself so she couldn't get past him. Ms. Hober-Stratman stopped and extended her head forward a little. She looked like a panther about to spring. That really should have been a warning to him, but he went on, undaunted.

"Always by yourself, Ms. Hober-Stratman. That isn't good. I'm beginning to worry about you. Besides, I'd welcome the chance to speak tête-à-tête about your little secret."

"Secret?" cried Ms. Hober-Stratman. "What's that supposed to mean?"

"Well now, you know how the faculty gossips. For instance, what was that I read in the paper a few weeks ago about you—or should I say, *by* you? Perhaps we could discuss it over dinner sometime. That would certainly be pleasanter than the teachers' lounge. Who knows who else might overhear?"

Ms. Hober-Stratman took a deep breath. "I do not wish, my dear Mr. Barnes, to discuss anything at all with you!" she bellowed at him so loud that everyone in the schoolyard turned to look. "Not in the teachers' room or at dinner or anywhere else!"

She shoved him out of her way and stalked off, her head held high, disappearing into the school.

Many of us had caught what had gone on between them. Appropriately embarrassed, Handsome Harry left the scene. Without looking around once, he ran into the school after Ms. Hober-Stratman. And so we were without supervision for the rest of the break.

"He knows something!" cried Collin once we'd recovered from our shock. "He definitely knows something! I've always suspected it. We're getting close, people! We're getting very close!"

Steffi, Radish, and I said nothing. We were too shocked. I'd been so happy for a few moments, and then that stupid Barnes comes along and spoils everything!

"Dude! What did he mean about the newspaper?"

"Are you really that dumb or are you just pretending?" Collin barked at me. "The article about the bank robbery! It was in the paper a few weeks ago. That's got to be what he was talking about!"

It wasn't true. It just couldn't be!

"Quick!" cried Collin. "Maybe there's something more going on inside!"

"Are you thinking of going into the building during break?" Radish asked in horror. "But you're not allowed!"

"The bio room is on the ground floor. We can look through the window! Maybe we'll find out something."

We ran over to the school, to the windows that belonged to our bio room. Carefully we peered in. But except for Charlie, our skeleton, there was nobody there.

Collin was visibly disappointed. "Too bad. I would have loved to know what Handsome Harry meant about the secret."

I'd been pretty sure for a while that I didn't want to know anything more at all. After the next break, I was positive.

Since we hadn't agreed ahead of time, we didn't go to our regular meeting place. Instead, we wandered aimlessly around the schoolyard.

After a few laps we ran into the guy from the

third period bio class who'd insulted Gorgeous the afternoon we followed Ms. Hober-Stratman to her apartment.

He picked up right where he left off. "What did you do with your toilet brush?" he called from a distance.

"If we sic the toilet brush on you, you'll look like Swiss cheese in two minutes!" Collin shot back.

The guy put his hands on his hips. "If you keep mouthing off, I won't tell you the big news."

"What big news?"

The guy grinned like a hyena. "Your field trip's been canceled."

"Dude! Why?"

"Hober-Stratman is gone."

"Baloney!" cried Steffi. "She just had outside supervision during the last break."

"I know, but we had her for bio last period. And the principal showed up instead of Hober-Stratman. And he said that she would be out *indefinitely*."

"Where'd she go?" asked Collin.

"No idea. I don't care, either."

He was about to go, but Radish held him back. "Is the field trip really so bad?"

"Duh! You saw how we looked when we came back."

"You had to run through the forest the whole day?"

"Yeah, the whole day. We only had one break—at a little hunting cabin. Hober-Stratman couldn't shut up about it. She raved on and on about the dump. Peace, quiet, and stuff like that. You're lucky to get out of it."

With that, he walked away.

"Dude! She can't just disappear! He's got to be lying!"

"I don't think so," said Collin. "He's much too dumb to make up a story like that. Besides, he wouldn't get anything out of it except trouble from us."

"Could she be sick?" Radish wondered.

"She still looked pretty healthy during the last break," said his sister.

Once again, our boss had a ready answer. "It must have something to do with Handsome Harry. For sure she's afraid he knows something about the bank robbery and probably intends to blackmail her. Maybe he's even in it with the guy from the café. And now she's taken off with the money. We'll probably never see her again!"

"Dude! You don't know that at all. Maybe she really is sick."

"Sure. And maybe there's a tooth fairy. Man, Norbert, can't you put two and two together?"

"We should at least go into the bio room once

more," suggested an uncharacteristically brave Radish. "Maybe she left a note on the blackboard. Teachers do that sometimes."

Collin was looking at Radish with frank admiration. "We're going to make a really good detective out of you some day, Radish. Let's go look. If anyone catches us, we'll think of an excuse."

Luckily, the bio room wasn't locked. The curtains were half drawn and it smelled stuffy. Charlie hung just opposite the door, grinning at us with his skeleton grin. A cold shudder ran down my spine.

"There's nothing on the board," Collin said, although we'd already seen that for ourselves. And at first nothing else struck us as unusual about our bio classroom.

But then, as we were on the way to the door, Steffi suddenly uttered an exclamation. I jumped. We weren't used to that from her.

She pointed at the windowsill. "Look what's sitting there!"

And then we saw it too. There on the windowsill sat Ms. Hober-Stratman's briefcase, right next to Charlie.

Collin reached it in one leap and picked it up.

"Dude! You aren't planning to take that, are you?"

"No, only look inside. After all, it's an emergency,

right? It's obvious she fled, terrified, when Handsome Harry exposed her, so she forgot the briefcase."

But one quick look in the briefcase was enough to learn that there was nothing exciting to be found in there.

"Bio homework, a notebook, and some stationery," Collin enumerated. "Odd. There aren't any personal things in here at all. No lipstick, no sandwich. Not even her class book!"

"All the same, she certainly didn't mean to leave her briefcase at school."

"Maybe she got sick so suddenly that she didn't think of it," said Radish.

Collin was dissatisfied with the meager findings. He took the homework papers out of the briefcase and looked inside again.

"Wait! There is something! A newspaper!"

"How exciting," Steffi sneered.

Ignoring her remark, he took out the newspaper and opened it up. He sucked in his breath as if he'd been bitten.

"What's the matter?" cried Steffi.

"Look at that! Look at that!"

Almost immediately, Steffi, Radish, and I were at his side, looking at the paper. In large black letters it said:

THIRD BANK ROBBERY!
SEVERAL HUNDRED THOUSAND $$$$ GRABBED!

Radish gasped for air. "But that's—"

"The article about the bank robbery," our boss finished. "In the briefcase of Ms. Hober-Stratman!"

Steffi shook her head. "I'm finally starting to believe that something's not right here."

This just could not be true!

"Dude! So what if she has the paper? A lot of people read the paper . . . I'm sure she's just out sick, the way the principal said."

"Why don't we simply go see her this afternoon and ask her?" Steffi suggested. "Then we'll know if she's sick or not. I, for one, would like to know what's wrong with her."

"You want to just go to her apartment, just like that?" asked Radish.

"What do you mean 'just like that'? Aren't you allowed to visit a sick teacher? It's perfectly normal."

"You think that's normal?" cried Collin. "Don't forget which teacher we're talking about here. I think the suggestion of going to visit her is good, but we have to come up with a better excuse."

"Then go ahead, Great Master."

Steffi always knows how to make Collin mad. "All

right!" he cried, his face red. "Fine! We'll meet at three o'clock at Gorgeous's place. By then I'll know how we can get our information discreetly. We'll just hang on to this newspaper for the moment. It can definitely be used in court as evidence."

In court! A knot formed in my stomach.

"Dude! Can I have the newspaper?"

"Why?"

"Because I have a good hiding place in my room."

Collin looked at me suspiciously for a long moment. But then he gave it to me. I just wanted to get it into a safe place for a while. If Ms. Hober-Stratman were actually charged, I could always decide then whether or not to give it to the police.

As I'd feared, I couldn't stop thinking about Ms. Hober-Stratman—not during the last two periods of school and not on the way home. The worst thing was that our suspicion that she could have something to do with the bank robbery was becoming more and more probable. All evidence pointed toward it, as Collin would say.

I knew I'd go crazy if I didn't find out soon what was going on, and it seemed like the most logical thing to just go and ask her. If only I weren't so afraid of doing it.

On the way to see Gorgeous, I thought about how often I was upset because the other members of Collin and Co. never really took me seriously. Even Radish had teased me a few times. But now I was glad I had them.

"So, what do you suggest?" Steffi greeted our boss, as soon as he arrived.

"Uh-well . . . I—" he stammered. "I've decided we're going to improvise."

"Sounds like a great plan," said Steffi, grinning.

I looked at the nameplates by the entrance door to the building where we'd seen Ms. Hober-Stratman.

"Dude! There's another name on it!"

HERMAN, W.

And underneath that was written with a ballpoint pen:

HOBER–STRATMAN, RING 2X

"Who might this Herman be?" I asked.

"We'll probably find out if you ring," said Steffi.

I carefully pressed the button two times. We waited a while, but nothing happened. I tried again. Again, nothing.

"She's probably not home," declared Radish, when nothing happened after the third attempt either.

"Then let's just try pressing once," Collin suggested. "Let's see what happens then."

I'd come so far already, I figured why not. I pressed the button firmly one time. It wasn't long before the door opener buzzed. Collin pushed the door open and went in. Steffi and Radish followed him, and I brought up the rear with Gorgeous in my arms.

We found the apartment that belonged to the bell right away. The same nameplate that was on the buzzer was affixed to the door:

HERMAN, W.

in big block letters, and under it

HOBER-STRATMAN

in ballpoint. But no one had opened the door.

"Should we knock?" Radish whispered.

Collin snorted. "Of course! Do you think I want to spend the night here?"

I knocked carefully on the glass that was set into the apartment door. It rattled as if I had kicked it. Suddenly, the door was thrown open, and standing before us was a woman like none I had ever seen before. She weighed at least two hundred pounds, although she wasn't especially tall. To make up for it, she had her hair piled up into a structure bearing a remarkable resemblance to the Leaning Tower of Pisa. Although she was certainly as old as my grandmother, there was a lot of makeup plastered on her face and her lips glowed rosy red.

"What do you want?" she asked us in a not very friendly way. "I'm not buying anything."

"We . . . um . . . aren't selling anything, either," began Collin, the master of improvisation.

"What?"

Collin opened his mouth, but nothing came out.

"I . . . um . . . we only want to collect money," he barely managed to get out.

I looked down at the trembling, whistling Gorgeous and had an inspiration.

"We're from the Society for Abused Animals. We need money for food."

The powder-caked face changed completely. It looked as if the sun had come out. "Animals! I love animals!"

"Are you Mrs. Herman?" asked Steffi from the back.

"Yes, Winnifred Herman! Do you know me, dear?"

"No, it's on your nameplate."

"May we come in for a moment?" I asked cautiously.

She looked at us skeptically for a second, then she took a step to one side and waved us in.

"Come right in, children! I have rarely visitors! Any change is welcome, at my age."

We went in and stood in the hallway. She looked at Gorgeous and shook her towering head. "Poor animal! Is that one of your protégés?"

Steffi didn't miss her opportunity. "Yes! He's our most needy case."

Gorgeous pressed closed to me and whistled as loud as he could—what an actor!

The woman's hand vanished into a pocket and came back into view with a change purse in it. Before I knew what was happening, she held some money under my nose. "Here, my boy! This should feed him for a while!"

My hand reached automatically for the money. I didn't really want to take it, but if I didn't, my whole cover would be blown.

"Many thanks!"

"No thanks necessary, my boy. I give gladly for a good cause."

Steffi was looking at Collin, but he still said nothing. So she finally got down to business. "Does Ms. Hober-Stratman also live with you?"

"Yes, she sublets from me. She lives here in the apartment in a furnished room. Do you want to collect from her, too?"

Sublets! Furnished room! This was getting more and more horrible. It was hard enough to believe that Ms. Hober-Stratman had an apartment in this building, much less that she lived here as a sub-tenant in a dusty furnished room. And she was supposed to be a bank robber? Perhaps she'd just become one out of desperation, in order to get out of here.

This time Steffi didn't lie. "No, she's our teacher. We wanted to ask her something."

"I'm sorry. She's not here."

"Not here?" I cried. I felt my heart suddenly beating faster. "She isn't sick, is she?"

"No, not as far as I know."

"Do you know when she'll be coming back? Or where she went?" Radish stayed on track.

"No, unfortunately I don't know that either. But now let's be honest, children. I may be old, but I'm not stupid. What's going on here? Why are you so keen to find your teacher?"

We looked at each other for a moment. None of us knew what to say.

Finally, our boss took over. "Today our principal said that Ms. Hober-Stratman might not be coming

114

back again, so we thought that she might be sick. But the thing is, we'd seen her a short time before, and she looked fine to us. So we came to find out what's wrong with her."

Mrs. Herman looked at Collin thoughtfully. "It makes sense. Today she came home from school much earlier than usual. But she didn't look sick, more like excited or nervous."

Collin rammed his elbow into my ribs. "Why was she nervous?" he asked right away. "Did she tell you that?"

"No, she only said that she was going away for a while."

"Really?" cried Steffi and Collin at the same time.

"Yes. Really," said Mrs. Herman with a smile. "And then she packed her bag and went."

"Any idea where?" I asked. My voice was trembling.

"I asked her that, too. But she only said that she had to get away."

"Didn't she leave any address behind?"

She shook her teetering hairdo. "No, she did not. We don't know each other that well, either. She's only lived here with me for three months."

"That's all? Do you know where she lived before?" Collin tried again.

"No, I don't know that either. But it must have been somewhere nearby, because when she moved in with me she brought her things in her own car. She went back and forth at least ten times."

I pulled all my courage together. "May we see her room?"

Mrs. Herman looked at me as though I had kicked her in the shins. "Now that's going too far, young man! You don't seriously think that I'm going to let you poke around in my tenant's room! If you want to know something, you must ask Ms. Hober-Stratman herself."

It was obvious our interview was over. Once more Collin played the great detective. "Many thanks, Mrs. Herman. You've really helped us with our investigation very much."

She smiled and tousled his hair, which immediately earned him a sly grin from Steffi.

"Don't mention it, my boy. And don't worry, everything is sure to have an entirely harmless explanation."

We were almost out the door when I realized I still had the money Mrs. Herman had given me for Gorgeous. I held it out to her.

She looked sympathetically at Gorgeous, whom I had picked up again. "No, why don't you keep it. He could use something extra between his ribs."

As soon as we were out on the street, Steffi pounced on Collin. "Fabulous improvisation, Boss. Really magnificent!"

"Yeah, yeah," he murmured. "Today wasn't really my best day. But all the same, we found out a lot."

"Dude! You call that a lot? We only know that she isn't sick and that she went somewhere."

"But why was she so secretive about it?" Collin asked.

"It's really quite simple. Would you tell everyone where you were going if you were on the lam and probably carrying a lot of money on you?" said Radish.

"If she really is on the lam, you could be right," Steffi agreed.

"Sure. And what's more, she may be hiding in a place that we already know," Collin continued.

"Dude! Do you mean the villa?"

"You get an A plus, Norbert. That's exactly what I think."

A Hunting Expedition
with Gorgeous

STEFFI, COLLIN, AND RADISH were excitedly discussing our interrogation of Mrs. Herman, but I wasn't listening to them. I was much too busy thinking about what Radish had said. On the lam! Was Ms. Hober-Stratman really running away from the police? Maybe she was there in the house with her husband and everything would turn out to have been a misunderstanding.

But just as we came within sight of the big house, the gate opened. The red sports car roared out of the driveway, its tires squealing, and disappeared around the next corner.

"Did you see who was in the car?" Collin asked.

"Dude! No way! He was much too fast."

"So, let's ring!" cried Collin. "Maybe Ms. Hober-Stratman's still there."

"And what if she isn't?" asked Radish. "What if somebody else answers?"

"Then we'll think of something," Collin answered with a sideways glance at Steffi.

We rang and were surprised when the gate opened once again after a short time. Before us stood a man who was easy to recognize as the gardener, probably because he had a rake in his hand.

The gardener looked at us inquiringly.

"Can you help us?" Steffi asked.

"I'll try. What's the matter?"

"Was that Mr. Hober who just drove away in the car?

"Yes, that was him. Why?"

"Was he alone?" Steffi asked back.

"I don't know. I was out behind the house when he drove away. But why do you ask?"

Before anyone could invent another dumb excuse, I decided to try the truth—most of it, at least. "We're looking for our teacher to talk to her about our classwork. She's related to Mr. Hober, you see. And we thought perhaps she might be here."

"Unfortunately, I can't help you there. I only know Mr. Hober."

"There's not a lady in the house?" asked Steffi.

"Not at the moment, as far as I know."

"Was there ever?" I asked. "Someone with black hair—and very pretty?" I just ignored the sneering looks of the others.

"Very pretty, huh?" said the gardener, laughing. "That certainly fits Mr. Hober's taste, but I've never yet seen a lady with black hair here. The ones who've crossed my path have all had blond hair."

We exchanged looks. I wondered whether Mr. Hober was a bigamist.

"But I've only been working here for the last few weeks. Maybe she was before my time," the gardener continued.

"No, no!" cried Collin. "She would have been here yesterday or today."

"Then I've definitely never seen her, but that isn't saying much. I only work here for a few hours in the afternoon. Sorry I can't help you any further."

"Can you then at least tell us where Mr. Hober was going?" I wanted to know.

"He only said to me that he would be away for a few days—a long weekend."

"He didn't say where?"

The gardener scratched his head. "Wait a minute. He did mention yesterday that he might be going to Huntsville this weekend."

I don't know how we managed to say good-bye and get around the next corner inconspicuously. "Huntsville!" cried Collin excitedly. "I don't believe it! The field trip!"

"Man, I bet I know where he is!" Steffi squealed. "The hunting cabin! Remember what the guy said at recess? That they took a break with Ms. Hober-Stratman there."

Collin nodded. "Peace and quiet. Except this time she is most certainly not there for that. They're going to divide the loot! Maybe after their fight at the café, the gangsters decided to kidnap her. You know, blackmailers will do anything for money!"

Again a cold shiver ran down my spine. "Dude! You don't seriously think he'd do anything bad to her!"

"We have to take that into consideration, Norbert."

"Collin, you've seen too many crime shows," Steffi was getting upset. "Quit scaring Norbert!"

"Are you so sure she isn't in danger, then?" Collin retorted. "And even if she's not, she still took off with the loot."

Steffi had nothing to say to that.

"Okay, so if we want to be certain, we have to find out."

"Then you intend to find the hunting cabin," Radish said.

"That's exactly what I intend to do. Unfortunately, it's too late today. But we don't want to lose any more time than necessary, so I figure the best thing would be for us to go tomorrow right after school."

On the way home, we stopped at the railroad station to find out how much a train ticket to Huntsville cost. When we put together all the money we had, we determined that it would just be enough.

"I was saving up to buy a comic book with that," Radish complained.

"Ms. Hober-Stratman is a whole lot more important than your dumb comic book," I barked at him.

Finally we looked at the timetable. We were in luck. A local train left for Huntsville at two o'clock. And one also came back again in the evening.

"Hopefully it won't take too long for us to find the way to the lodge and hopefully it isn't too far," said Radish anxiously. "The last train back leaves at seven."

"So?" Collin asked in irritation. "The trip takes half an hour. That means we're there around two-thirty. Then we have four hours left for our operation. That's sure to be enough!"

"Then there's nothing more in the way of our hunting expedition," said Steffi. "And we'll also have our hunting dog right there."

After school the next day I really had to hurry. The train left at two o'clock and I still had to pick up Gorgeous.

"My goodness, Norbert!" Mom scolded. "Don't gobble your food so. It looks as though you hadn't eaten in three days."

"I have to hurry," I answered with my mouth full.

She smiled. "Are you meeting your detective friends again?"

I just nodded. Luckily, she didn't ask anything more. It was no fun to lie to her—besides, she usually caught me right away. On my way out, I got something out of my hiding place in my closet. I could still decide later if I was going to use it.

I just made it. The train was already waiting at the platform. Steffi, Radish, and Collin were standing beside it and waving to me excitedly. I ran as fast as I could with Gorgeous in my arms.

"We thought we were going to have to leave without you for sure."

"Couldn't get here any sooner," I gasped. "And it was faster to carry Gorgeous than to let him run alongside me. He stops at every lamp post."

Unfortunately we couldn't find an empty compartment, so we sat with an old married couple who stared at us the whole trip. Gorgeous, especially, seemed to be a problem for them. A few times the woman looked at him and wrinkled her nose.

"Should we ask about the cabin right at the railroad station?" I asked Collin.

But he only shook his head and put his index finger to his lips. He was right. You can't discuss criminal cases around people like that.

"It was my plan to ask the people at the station, too," Collin explained to me when we finally got off. "Preferably locals."

Since Steffi, Radish, and I had no idea how to recognize locals, we let Collin take the lead. However, that didn't get us much further. No one seemed to know of a hunting cabin in the vicinity. A friendly old man who probably didn't understand so well what we wanted first told us the way to the church, then to the hospital, and finally to an old forester's house.

"We aren't going to get anywhere this way," Collin admitted in disappointment.

"I'd rather just go back home again," Steffi complained.

"No! We're here now, so we'll keep on looking.

We have to wait until seven o'clock anyway. There's no train back any earlier."

"Well, it's all right with me. But I don't want to keep on asking people. It's embarrassing."

"Dude! The old man told us something about a forester's house. We could try going there."

Collin looked at me as if I'd lost my marbles. "What do you want there? We're looking for a hunting cabin. Hey, why don't we also go to the hospital. The old man told us the way there, too."

"Think about it for a minute, smart guy! If the forester doesn't know where a hunting cabin is in his forest, who would?"

"Sure!" cried Radish. "We'll ask the forester. And if he doesn't know either, then we can go back home."

Collin still wasn't convinced, but he was overruled. So we got started on the path the old man had described to us.

We didn't have to walk far before we got to the forest. I let Gorgeous run, for which he was grateful. As he barked wildly and hopped around, I looked at my watch. It was almost four o'clock. The inquiries in the station had cost us a lot of time.

Collin had seen my glance at my wrist. "No problem, Norbert. We still have time. We're in the forest already, so it can't be much farther."

He was mistaken. When we finally discovered the old forester's house, my feet felt as if they were on fire.

"Finally!" Radish groaned too. "It's about time. I was thinking we were lost."

Collin hadn't minded the long hike. At least, that's how he acted. "My goodness! A little hike like that through the woods is nothing! And we certainly won't get lost, as long as I'm here."

"There's a car there!" Steffi interrupted him. "But it isn't Ms. Hober-Stratman's."

In front of the little house, which was at least a hundred years old, stood a large, flashy car with fat tires and a spoiler.

"Status-mobile," murmured Collin. "Is the guy next to it the forester?"

He didn't look particularly confidence-inspiring. I would much sooner have believed him to be a bank robber.

"The car matches him," Steffi whispered to me. As a precaution, I picked Gorgeous up.

The guy came toward us, beaming as if we were old friends.

"Ah!" he cried. "You're sure to be the Broadfield children! And where are your parents?"

"At home," said Steffi, without batting an eyelash.

Flashy Car looked at us with an unbelievably dumb face. "What? I don't understand. But your parents wanted——"

"I think you have us confused with someone else," said Collin, interrupting him. "Our name isn't Broadfield."

"Oh. Then I must be mistaken," he declared, still grinning. "Are you out for a walk?"

"No," Collin answered. "We're looking for the forester's house."

Flashy Car's face became a degree dumber. "The forester's house? And your parents are at home?"

Collin nodded. "All correct."

Suddenly the guy started waving his hands around. "No, no! You must get your parents. I can't show you the house without your parents."

"Dude! Are you the forester, or what?"

Mr. Flashy Car laughed, showing teeth so white they glittered. "Do I look like a forester? No, I'm a real estate agent. I'm selling the forester's house. And the Broadfields wanted to look at it."

"Then no one's living here at the moment."

"It's empty, if you don't count a few mice," the agent cackled.

"Do you perhaps know of a hunting cabin around here somewhere?" Steffi inquired.

The agent scratched his head. "Yes," he said then.

127

"There is a hunting cabin around here. It's not far away, as I recall. But I'm not exactly sure where it is—I passed it once by chance."

We thanked him and quickly made tracks out of there.

"I wouldn't want to meet him in a dark alley," said Radish when we were out of view.

"I wouldn't either," Collin agreed. "But at least we know there is a hunting cabin around here somewhere. I'd almost stopped believing we'd ever find it."

"We haven't found it yet," said Steffi. "We only know it exists . . . not the way there. I'm for turning around."

Collin looked at his watch. "We used up half an hour at the forester's house. We still have almost two hours to look for the lodge."

"And how do you intend to find the way, smart aleck?"

Now was the time to put my plan into action. I thought for a moment, then opened my jacket to pull out what I'd brought from home.

"What is that?" cried Steffi.

"Dude! Isn't it obvious? It's Ms. Hober-Stratman's wig!"

"Where'd you get it?"

"I got it out of the ladies' room in the café."

"Oh, so you went back for it," said Steffi with

that taunting undertone in her voice that we all knew so well. "What did you want it for?"

Luckily, I'd had enough time to think up a good excuse. "As evidence. I thought it might come in handy, and I was right. We'll let Gorgeous sniff it, and then he can pick up Ms. Hober-Stratman's scent and lead us to her. Now you'll see how useful Gorgeous can be to us."

"Fantastic, Norbert." Collin was looking at me admiringly. "Hold the thing under his nose!"

"I hope he doesn't eat it," said Steffi.

He didn't. He sniffed at it curiously. Then he turned his head to the side and looked around, as if he were searching for something.

I stretched out my arm. "Go, Gorgeous! Find Ms. Hober-Stratman!"

For a second he looked at me questioningly, but then he seemed to understand. He took off in the direction in which I had pointed. I quickly stuffed the wig under my jacket again before Collin got the idea of taking it away from me.

"After him!" cried Collin and was already running. Radish and I ran after him.

"I hope this turns out all right," I heard Steffi say behind me.

Gorgeous led us back and forth through the forest. Sometimes he ran purposefully along a path as if he'd actually picked up the scent of Ms. Hober-Stratman. But then he would leap around between the trees again, sniffing here, sniffing there, as if he didn't exactly know what he was really supposed to be doing. I tried to fix the path in my head as well as I could. But that wasn't so easy. Forest paths look very similar to each other.

"I've had it now!" Steffi cried suddenly. "I'll bet my next allowance that he has no idea what he's doing. Let's go back."

But Collin was in the grip of hunting fever. "He's very close. I'm totally certain!"

I looked at my watch. My heart almost slipped into my throat with horror. "It's almost six!"

The others looked at their watches. They'd forgotten the time, just like me.

"Now we have to get back fast!" cried Steffi. "If we don't catch the last train, we'll have to spend the night on a park bench."

Collin remained cool. "No problem. I remember the way. We'll do it easily."

I picked up Gorgeous again and we went back in the opposite direction. At first, we seemed to be making progress. But soon we started seeing the same landmarks over and over.

Finally, even Collin had to admit, "We're lost, people."

Radish let himself fall on the moss with a groan. We all sat down next to him.

"So what are we going to do now?" I asked, although I knew no one had an answer to that.

"It's almost a quarter to seven. We'll never make the train now!"

Steffi was right. In my mind I saw us wandering through the forest in the middle of the night. The only thing that reassured me was that I wasn't alone.

"Our parents are going to be so worried," said Radish quietly.

When I thought about that, my insides contracted. Mom worries so much about me anyway. Because I'm alone so often, she says. If I didn't come home tonight, she would certainly go crazy with worry. If only we'd never started on this search for this stupid hunting cabin. Why did we have to stick our noses into Ms. Hober-Stratman's life? If only we'd left her in peace! Or if only I hadn't betrayed her! But why did she just abandon us—surely she must have known how much she meant to me! The longer I thought about it, the angrier I became.

"Dude! What a mess! We should have marked the trail!"

"Or dropped bread crumbs along the way, like Hansel and Gretel!"

Even in this situation Steffi had to make her dumb jokes.

Collin had other concerns. "Bread crumbs! Cut it out! I could eat a whole cow, I'm so hungry."

"How can you think about eating?" Steffi screamed at him suddenly. "Instead, how about thinking about getting us out of this forest! After all, you got us into this mess! And in an hour it's going to be dark!"

"You think I don't want to get out of here as fast as possible?" Collin screamed back. "But I can still be hungry! And besides, it was Norbert's idea to let Gorgeous track!"

I couldn't believe what I was hearing. "Dude! Are you nuts? You were totally thrilled with the idea! It was a stroke of genius, you said. And now I'm to blame for everything? I can't believe this!"

The three of us went back and forth like this for a while. Only Radish said nothing. He sat with his legs crossed on the moss, staring into the distance. I figured he was in such despair that he couldn't utter a word. But I was very much mistaken about that.

Suddenly he bellowed into the midst of it all, "Could you all please shut up? I have to think! A person can't think clearly when you're carrying on like a bunch of babies."

Collin stopped short in the middle of a blast of rage at me, and Steffi and I fell silent at once.

Although Radish and Steffi are twins, they couldn't be more different from one another. Aside from the fact that they look completely different, Steffi doesn't take anything seriously. She laughs about everything and everyone, and she can spark the biggest fights in the shortest possible time with her biting remarks—which Radish then tries to settle again. Radish hates fighting. He always tries to get along well with everyone, and he worries about everything. His anxiety has often slowed down our boss, which isn't necessarily a bad thing. Who knows what trouble he might have gotten us into otherwise? So it was funny that Radish, of all people, was the only one who kept his nerve when the rest of us were so scared our knees were knocking.

"Do you have an idea?" Collin asked carefully.

He answered with another question. "When we came into the forest it was just about four o'clock, right?"

"Pretty close. Why?"

"Can any of you remember where the sun was when we came into the forest?" Radish persisted.

"Directly in front of us," Steffi answered immediately. "It was almost blinding me the whole way to the forester's house. I know that for sure."

She was right. I could remember that now, too.

"Good," Radish said. "At three-thirty the sun had already passed its highest position. We must therefore have been going west, since it goes down there. If we now go in the opposite direction, we'll hit the town again. We just have to make sure that we always have the sun at our backs."

Collin was looking at Radish as if he'd seen a ghost. "Man, Radish! Crazy!"

We stood up and looked back at the sun. Luckily, it was still high enough in the sky for us to be able to see the direction. Of course, we had to beat our way straight through the forest—the trails wound around too much—but none of us minded that.

Collin turned the lead over to Radish without argument. Steffi and I walked behind the two of them. When I looked over at her, she said softly, "My brother." And she was beaming as she said it.

Wordlessly, we tramped through the forest. We took turns carrying Gorgeous. No one complained about it, not even Collin. We were at the end of our strength. I'd have preferred to lie down somewhere and sleep. The farther we went, the smaller our hope became that we'd still make it before dark. The sun crept behind the trees and sank lower and lower.

But then something happened that none of us were expecting.

"There's a house!" Radish cried suddenly. And then the rest of us saw it, too.

"Dude! That's no house! That's a hunting cabin!"

We could just barely make out the little wooden cabin in the dusky light. But the nearer we got, the more clearly we saw that I was right. It was a hunting cabin. It was set in a small clearing that was illuminated by the last beams of the sun—and there was a red sports car parked in front of the door.

Night of Truth

COLLIN WAS THE FIRST to recover from the shock. "We have to check it out!" he hissed. "But quietly!"

As we were sneaking closer to the cabin, I couldn't get Steffi's dumb joke about Hansel and Gretel out of my mind. Without wanting to, I was forced to think about the witch and the oven. Only I didn't know if Ms. Hober-Stratman was Gretel or the witch. Suddenly I was so afraid that something had happened to her, I felt like calling her name aloud. I was completely lost in my thoughts and was startled when all at once we were standing at the back wall of the cabin.

Now that it was once again a matter of solving the Hober-Stratman case, Collin resumed command.

"We have to get up to a window without being seen," he whispered. "Maybe we can see in."

We slipped around the cabin. Three sides were enclosed by a high privacy fence. There was a garden gate, of course, but that was as high as the privacy fence and had boards nailed over it. Only the back wall was open. And there there was only one window, which was covered with shutters. When we got to the other side of the cabin, Collin stopped suddenly. "Man, there's another car parked there! But I've never seen that one!"

We saw it too. It looked new.

"Now who could that belong to?" Radish whispered.

"No idea," Collin answered. "The guy from the café, maybe . . . But be quiet for a minute. Maybe we'll hear something."

We crouched under the window at the back of the cabin and listened, but the only thing we heard was Gorgeous's excited whistling.

"Can't that animal ever stop squeaking?" said Collin in irritation.

I held his muzzle closed. Then he began to whine, and that was louder than the whistling. I let go of him and tried not to pay any attention to the whistling. It took a while until we could hear muffled voices from the inside of the cabin.

"There are at least two," Collin declared unnecessarily.

The longer we listened, the clearer it became that the two voices were arguing. They kept getting louder, but not clearer.

"Dude! I can't make out anything. Do you understand what it's about?"

"I think I heard something about money," said Radish.

"Really?" said Collin, much too loud. But the voices inside the cabin were apparently so busy with their argument that they didn't notice any noises from the outside.

"I can't hear anything at all," said Steffi. "I can't even tell if one of the voices belongs to Ms. Hober-Stratman. If only the shutters weren't there!"

But then we suddenly heard a woman's voice. "I've had enough of this! Either we have it for ourselves alone or not at all!"

"Did you hear that?" whispered Collin. "She's got to mean the loot."

At the same moment the front door was flung open. Luckily, we were standing at the back wall. We dropped to the ground as if on cue. When I looked up, I could clearly make out a woman with blond hair. It was the supermodel we'd encountered at the mansion.

"So she's in on it, too," whispered Collin. "I might have known."

She stomped angrily to the red car, ripped open the door on the driver's side, and got behind the steering wheel. Shortly afterward a man came after her. And we knew him too. It was Mr. Hober. He was running after the supermodel. "Now listen to me!" he cried. "She certainly didn't mean it like that. Why shouldn't we simply divide it among us?"

"Leave me alone!" the peroxide blond shrieked. "All or nothing. You promised me!"

Mr. Hober looked back at the cabin and shrugged his shoulders. Then he climbed into the passenger seat. With engine howling and tires spinning, the beautiful red sports car dashed away.

I'd gotten used to the quiet in the forest for the past several hours, so the sound of the engine seemed much louder to me than it actually was. It rapidly got softer and softer.

"Now it's all clear," Collin whispered. "They've been arguing about the loot, so the money must still be in the cabin."

"Is anyone still in there?" Radish wanted to know.

"Man, little brother! There has to be at least one still in there. They didn't look as though they'd been fighting with each other. Besides, the other car is still parked by the door."

"I just wonder whether that someone is Ms. Hober-Stratman," I added.

We stood up. At that moment we heard a noise behind the privacy fence. It was a horrible cracking and crunching and knocking. In my fright, I dropped Gorgeous, who landed on the ground whining and whistling

"Dude! What's that? It sounds really horrible!"

Collin wiped the pine needles off his trousers as if he wasn't at all interested in the grisly noises. "They're probably hiding the loot. I have to see! Can someone lift me up?"

Steffi tapped her forehead. "Lift you up? You must be nuts!"

Have I mentioned that Collin is at least a half a head taller than the rest of us and he isn't exactly built small, either?

"Radish is the lightest one of all of us. Let's lift him up to see over the gate," I suggested.

Radish looked at me in horror. "Me? And what if they see me?"

"They won't," said our boss. "They're much too busy with their loot."

"And who's supposed to lift me up?" asked Radish, his voice trembling.

Steffi answered immediately, "Collin."

"All right, then, get up on my shoulders, Radish."

Radish has just about as much skill at sports as I do, so he needed a few attempts before he was finally, with all our help, shakily standing on Collin's shoulders. Then Collin, with Radish on his shoulders, placed himself in front of the gate so that Radish could look over. Gorgeous was no great help to us, either. He jumped around between our legs and whistled through the gaps in his teeth. Still, somehow we managed not to be noticed.

Finally, Radish was able to look over the privacy fence, but the minute he did, he screamed as if Dracula were lurking behind it. Collin jumped and they both began to sway dangerously. Radish continued to scream and Collin managed to run two steps before he tipped over and Radish landed in the moss with a loud cry.

"There's a murderer there!" he yelled when he'd scrambled to his feet. "A murderer with a mask and an ax! And there's still blood on it!" He was pointing with outstretched arm and trembling hand to the gate over which he'd just looked.

Then the garden gate was torn open and the murderer rushed over to us. However, in his excitement and the poor light, Radish had made a mistake. The mask was a hunting cap, and although the man did have an ax in his hand, there was no blood on it—half the blade was covered with red paint.

The face that was discernible under the cap was one I knew. "The man from the café!" I cried.

I'd seen his face only once, briefly. But that had been enough for it to imprint itself on my mind forever.

It had all happened very fast. We were still standing—well, Collin was sitting—petrified and hardly daring to breathe. The man just looked from one to the other of us in amazement. At that moment, the door to the hunting cabin opened and someone I knew even better came out: Ms. Hober-Stratman!

"Careful!" cried Radish, still beside himself. "He has an ax!"

"Of course I have an ax," the man remarked. "I was chopping wood. You need an ax for that."

He turned around to Ms. Hober-Stratman. "Do you know these children?"

She recognized us at once, but she needed a while to pull herself together after the surprise.

"What in the world . . . how the dickens did you get here . . . and how did you know . . ." she stammered. Her mouth kept opening and closing like a beached fish.

We looked at one another. No one dared say anything. But then we all began to talk at the same time, everything coming out a jumbled mess. At least it must have sounded like that to Ms. Hober-Stratman.

"Stop!" she shouted over our babble. "Come inside first. You can't see your hand in front of your face out here."

She went ahead, we followed her, and the man with the ax brought up the rear. He hadn't said anything at all up until then, only smiled.

The cabin consisted of a single room. It was quiet in there, even quieter than it had been in the forest before. In one corner there was a fire burning in the fireplace. The man from the café had probably been chopping wood for that.

We sat beside each other on a sofa. Ms. Hober-Stratman looked at us in silence, shaking her head now and then. I don't know how long we'd been sitting there on the sofa not knowing where to look until finally she said to the man, "By the way, these are my students."

"I'd already figured that."

"Are you going to rub us out now?" Collin asked, suddenly panic-stricken.

"Are we going to do *what*?" asked Ms. Hober-Stratman, her eyes widening.

"We won't tell on you!" cried Collin, completely beside himself.

"Tell me, Collin, did you bump your head on a tree when you were running through the woods?"

"I think these kids think we're doing dark dealings here," observed Radish's murderer, who hadn't stopped smiling.

"Dude! You're not, are you Ms. Hober-Stratman? You and your accomplice—I mean friend—are just having a vacation here, right?"

"Accomplice? Really, Norbert!"

"Or is it your husband?"

Ms. Hober-Stratman's eyes grew even wider.

"Accomplice! Husband! I've had just about enough of this!" cried Ms. Hober-Stratman. Then she looked at her watch. "It's already after eight. Do your parents have any idea where you are?"

We said nothing. It wasn't necessary.

"Aha. I thought so. I'll drive you home. At once!"

The way she said it, none of us dared to contradict her. Our teacher was back, that was for sure. She looked at the man from the café and raised her eyebrows questioningly.

"It's all right with me," he said. "It doesn't matter now, anyway."

"We can drive back again," said Ms. Hober-

144

Stratman. And then she smiled at him! A love smile . . . it was like a stab in the heart.

She stood up and herded us out to her car without another word.

"I hope they really intend to drive us home," Collin whispered to me. Luckily, the radio was on, otherwise Ms. Hober-Stratman would probably have heard him.

However, Radish *had* heard. "Where else would they drive us?"

Collin didn't answer that, but we knew what he meant.

Ms. Hober-Stratman drove, the man with the ax sat in the passenger seat, and Collin, Steffi, Radish, and I had squeezed into the backseat with Gorgeous on my lap.

The road through the forest was pitch black, and more a track than a road. "She's certainly driving deeper and deeper into the forest," Collin murmured. "Where no one will hear our screams."

I felt sick. Why was Collin trying to freak us all out? I wanted to plug my ears.

The ride through the dark forest seemed to last an eternity. My fear was growing as the minutes ticked by. But then I saw lights. It was a lighted main road. Then, after a few hundred feet, she stopped in front of a telephone booth and went into it.

"Dude! Who do you think she's calling?" I whispered.

"Her accomplices. She wants to discuss what to do with us," Collin whispered back.

"Will you shut up!" Steffi hissed.

If Collin was right, Ms. Hober-Stratman and her accomplices quickly agreed.

"So," she said, almost relieved, when she was sitting behind the steering wheel again, "I reached your mother, Norbert. She said I should bring you all to her. You can all stay overnight at your apartment. She'll call the other parents and tell them. You have a very nice mother, Norbert."

I looked at Collin. "Idiot!"

A shrug was his only answer. On the day he admits he's wrong, I'll buy Gorgeous a big filet mignon.

"Fantastic!" Steffi rejoiced. "Then we'll finally get to see where you live, Norbert."

I barely had one problem solved, when along came a new one. Now everyone would see where I lived. At the moment, though, I almost didn't care. If they didn't like it, they didn't have to come back.

Without any attempt to "rub us out," as Collin had feared, Ms. Hober-Stratman drove straight to my front door.

The first thing Mom noticed when we climbed

up the stairs was Gorgeous. She didn't have to say anything—her look was enough for me.

"We're keeping him in Collin's aunt's garden!" I cried right away. "We all take care of him together!"

Mom smiled. "Well, good. As long as he stays out of the apartment."

I was too happy. And you know what happens when you get too happy—you make mistakes. At least that's how it always is with me. While we were still standing in the hall, I did a very dumb thing: I took off my jacket. Before I could grab it, the wig fell to the floor. Everyone stared at it.

"Where did you get that?" cried Ms. Hober-Stratman. I couldn't look at her face to see if she was angry or ashamed. I was paralyzed. Why hadn't I kept the stupid jacket on? I had never wished so hard to be able to undo something.

Mom noticed at once that something was wrong and quickly tried to come to my rescue.

"Norbert will certainly explain that to us soon, but first let's all go into the living room."

She made cocoa for us, and coffee for the grown-ups. She told us that she'd dug out a few old sleeping bags for Collin, Radish, and Steffi to sleep in.

"Your mother is really cool," Radish whispered to me as we sat at the table sipping our cocoa.

"That's right," said Collin. "We should come here more often."

Suddenly it was clear to me how much I'd underestimated my friends.

"Well, now I want to know why you were running around in some forest half an hour away, and what it has to do with this wig."

I told Mom the same story I'd already told her once about Ms. Hober-Stratman, leaving out our suspicions about the bank robbery.

When I was finished, Mom looked at Ms. Hober-Stratman. "The children were apparently really concerned about you. Norbert talks about you all the time."

Ms. Hober-Stratman looked at me in astonishment. "Really? I'm honored."

Collin rammed his elbow into my ribs. "Why didn't you just put the whole thing in the newspaper?"

I didn't care what Collin said. Ms. Hober-Stratman was honored! I was walking on air!

"Nevertheless, I don't understand. Why all the concern about me?"

I looked at the others, pleading with my eyes for help. Collin understood right away. "It was all so strange, Ms. Hober-Stratman. You had always dressed like all the other teachers and come to school in a regular old car. Then suddenly you were wearing cool clothes and makeup, and driving a sports car."

"That was what concerned you?"

"Not entirely," added Radish. "Then you were suddenly riding a bike . . . and there was your fight with Handsome Har— uh, Mr. Barnes."

"And then, on top of everything, Norbert saw you in the wig! And we followed you because we wanted to know what you were up to!"

When Steffi mentioned the wig, Ms. Hober-Stratman's eyes widened in shock, but she collected herself immediately.

"Perhaps you should just tell the children what really happened," Mom suggested.

Ms. Hober-Stratman looked around at all of us. "No," she said then. "I hate talking about my private life."

"Perhaps I can help," said the man with the ax.

"You?" she cried.

"Yes. Because I think you owe it to the children. After all, they got lost in the forest on your account. They must have gone through a terrible ordeal."

Collin started to protest, but Steffi kicked him under the table.

"Very well," she consented. "But only the most essential details, please."

Café Man cleared his throat. "First of all, the matter of the car and the bicycle is simple: her old car gave up the ghost and the new one required a few days' wait."

"Is that the one we came home in?" Radish interjected.

"Precisely. Anyway, that's why Bea, I mean Ms. Hober-Stratman, rode the bicycle."

Bea, what a beautiful name . . .

"Or she borrowed her brother's car."

"Brother?" Collin and I cried at the same time. "Mr. Hober is your brother?"

Ms. Hober-Stratman started. "How do you know my brother?"

"Then you aren't married?" I asked without thinking.

"Why do you ask?"

"Because of the names."

"When I married I took my husband's name, Stratman, and hyphenated."

"Dude! Then you *are* married! So who is he?" I pointed to Café Man.

They looked at each other.

"Very well," said Ms. Hober-Stratman, sighing. "I'll tell you, but then that's it! I will never talk about it again. Do you understand?"

We nodded politely.

"I grew up here. But after I got married, I moved away with my husband. Unfortunately, our marriage broke up."

I looked at Mom. She looked over at me at the same moment.

"After my divorce, I came back again," Ms. Hober-Stratman continued. "I was lucky to get a position in the school right away. I lived at my brother's house for a while—it's big enough, certainly. But then I took a furnished room in the same neighborhood as the school.

"But it wasn't so easy. I was lonely, but I had no desire to go to a disco like a sixteen-year-old and there wasn't anybody in my circle of acquaintances. And I wasn't about to get involved with any of my fellow teachers."

She hesitated for a moment. It was obviously hard for her to keep on talking. I felt like telling her to stop, but I was too curious to do that.

"Oh, well, anyway," she finally continued, "I decided to take matters into my own hands. I paid more attention to my appearance, went out once in a while, and finally—I put a personal ad in the paper."

"Dude! Honest?" I cried. It just sort of slipped out. Ms. Hober-Stratman looked at me—and blushed! If I could have, I would have run away.

"What's so unusual about that?" Mom said suddenly. "I've done that, too."

"You?" I cried. "Are you kidding?"

"Most certainly not. But it was a while ago, and it didn't turn up Mr. Right either."

"You can say that again!" Ms. Hober-Stratman said, visibly relieved. "You just cannot imagine what sort of guys you meet that way. Besides, I was always afraid that someone from school would see me during one of those embarrassing meetings."

"Is that why you wore the wig?" Collin asked curiously.

"Yes. Now I realize how silly it was. Especially when I had to keep wearing it when I actually got to know someone with whom I got along very well."

She gave Café Man the love smile again!

"Jordan kept telling me to take off that ridiculous wig, as he called it. But I was so possessed by the fear that someone might be snooping around in my private life that I couldn't do it. Several days ago we had our first real fight about it."

"That was in the café," Steffi whispered to me. Too loud, unfortunately.

"Aha. So you know about that, too?"

We were silent.

"Well, be that as it may, I was really angry. But

then I just decided I was being paranoid and so I threw the wig away."

I was gradually becoming brave. "But then why did you disappear so suddenly?"

Ms. Hober-Stratman gave me a withering look.

"Somehow a few other teachers found out that I was placing ads," she continued. "They'd already been gossiping about it for a while. But then when one of them actually said something to my face about it, I'd finally had enough. I reported in sick, and called Jordan and we drove to the hunting cabin. It belongs to my parents. But wouldn't you know, on this weekend, of all weekends, my brother and his girlfriend decided to go there, too. Needless to say, there was an argument when they showed up."

"Your brother's girlfriend behaved like a child!" cried Jordan. "I was so angry about it, I went out to let off steam by chopping wood. That's when I met you kids."

"Then Ms. Hober-Stratman *was* playing hookey after all!" cried Collin.

Ms. Hober-Stratman smiled. "Okay, Collin, you're right. But you promised at the cabin that you wouldn't tell."

"I'll keep the promise," said Collin. "Although, when I made it, I was talking about the bank robbery."

For such a smart guy, Collin can sure be dumb sometimes. Of course, he realized what he'd said—but too late.

Ms. Hober-Stratman looked at him in surprise, as Mom burst out laughing.

"I think I know what's going on! I told Norbert a few days ago about the bank robbery that took place right here in the neighborhood. The paper said that a woman took part in it and that the robbers were wearing wigs."

Ms. Hober-Stratman gasped. "And so the children thought—"

She got no further, for at that moment peals of laughter rang out. Collin, Steffi, Radish, and I sat there, not believing our eyes and ears. Our teacher—our very serious teacher—was doubled over, howling.

"But there was the newspaper, too!" cried Collin.

"What newspaper?" asked Ms. Hober-Stratman, wiping the tears from her eyes.

"We found it in your briefcase! You left it in the bio room, but at the time, we didn't know whose it was so we looked inside," I lied, before Collin could cause more mischief. "And the newspaper was in it—the one with the article about the bank robbery."

"Do you still have that paper?" asked the man who stole Ms. Hober-Stratman from me.

I looked at Collin.

He nodded and said, "Go get it."

Since neither Steffi nor Radish said anything, either, I ran into my room and dug the paper out of its hiding place.

"Now, open it to the next-to-last page," said Ms. Hober-Stratman with an odd smile.

I did. There were the personal ads!

"And now please read the ad that is underlined."

I had to clear my throat a few times before I could finally read:

TEACHER, AGE 30, SENSE OF HUMOR, LIKES SPORTS, NATURE LOVER, WOULD LIKE TO BE ADORED BY MORE THAN PUPILS.

What did she mean by that?

"Is that your ad?" cried Collin.

All we got in reply was that silly laughter again.

"I'm sorry we disappointed you so," chortled Jordan, the nature lover.

Collin stood up. "Come on, let's go into Norbert's room."

He didn't have to say that twice. When I shut the door behind us, the grown-ups were still laughing.

We talked for a long time about why things are so unfair in this world and why we have so much bad luck with our cases. Ms. Hober-Stratman and her friend hung around, chatting with my mom until late. Sometimes we heard them laughing—probably at us.

I was really disappointed that Ms. Hober-Stratman had a boyfriend, but I was glad it had all ended so harmlessly and I wouldn't have to testify against her in court after all.

As I was falling asleep, I thought about how nice it was that my friends were staying overnight with me for the first time; even Gorgeous was allowed to stay, just this once. That night I dreamed that Collin and Co. solved a real case in our next adventure.